By: Michelle Turner

Copyright 2012 Michelle Turner

Cover photo by Eden Crane Design

Edited by Jaidis Shaw

Dedication

Michele T., Emily T., Mindy B. & Melly R.: I can't thank you all enough for putting up with me while I was writing. You all supported me and encouraged me every step of the way. And I will never forget that.

Coconut: Thank you for putting up with cranky Mommy when I was in my writing mode and I promise we'll play SpongeBob Monopoly now that it's done. Mommy loves you more than the moon and the stars in the sky.

Gary Michael: You've showed me support and understanding through this whole process. Even when it involved you fixing dinner or eating take out because I couldn't pry myself away from writing. I'm blessed to call you my husband. I love you Monkey Butt.

Chapter 1- Bloom

~ I'm going to count the tearless days as small victories against the aching hole in my chest ~

I slowly pry my eyes open to stare at the stars stuck to my ceiling. They've been there since I was a kid. Dad helped me stick them up; over a 1000 little glow in the dark stars. They're my form of a night light. Seeing them brings back the memories just like everything else in this house, memories I can't face without crying. I pull the cover back over my head determined to go back to sleep. I know I need to face the day and I will face it, but knowing that today marks a year since I lost him makes it harder. There are days I wake up and just wish I could lay back down and sleep my life away. Today is one of those days.

Adam Michael Daniels was my Dad and he was also my best friend. He was always a hard worker; even when he was exhausted and knew he needed to rest he would still agree to work over. That's what eventually killed him. The police told me he fell asleep behind the wheel and ran off the road, right into a tree. He had just got off working a double for the third day in a row at the local factory. I tried to blame myself for the accident. I was determined he hadn't fallen asleep but that it was my car. He had been driving it to test out my brakes, but the sheriff explained that there wasn't even a sign he tried to brake. He drove full speed right off the road and out of my life.

Dad is the one who named me Bloom Michael; and he was the only parent I had. Even though he worked way too hard he always found time for me. He never missed a school event when I was growing up and he regularly took me fishing at the lake. I know I probably should've missed having my mother but I never felt that way. I loved having my Dad and I had a feeling that if she had been around I would've turned out completely different and not in a good way. Plus, you can't miss someone you don't even remember.

The woman people refer to as my mom left us when I was a day old. I have no memory of her, except what people have tried to tell me. Her name was Rose and apparently she told the nurses at the hospital she wanted to take a walk and never came back. Dad later found a note at the house from her stating she felt trapped and wasn't ready to be what we needed. From what my Dad's friends have told me he took it hard, but he held it in and didn't let it stop him from caring for me. With a little bit of help from them, he found a way to care for his new born while his heart was broken (his heart never really healed). I think he always thought she'd come back. He didn't even get rid of the things she had left behind. He kept them in his closet until I was old enough to start asking questions and then he moved them to our storage shed so I wouldn't have to see them.

When I turned 13 Dad gave me a necklace; a little white gold cross that was encrusted with diamonds. I loved it until I found out it had belonged to Rose. I know now that he just wanted me to have something that belonged to her, but at the time I was furious. I was convinced he was trying to turn me into her, which was the last thing I wanted. It was the first big fight we had. I didn't speak to him for almost a week. I wish now I could have that week back and tell him I realize what he was trying to do with that necklace. But I'll never get the chance.

Everyone has always told me I look more like Rose's clone than her child, though I never consider myself "her child." In my opinion she is only the surrogate that brought me to my Dad. But that doesn't change the fact that I have her heart-shaped face and butterscotch blonde hair that falls half way down my back. I stand around five foot seven just like I've been told she did. The only thing I received from my Dad in the looks department was his hazel eyes. Which happen to be my favorite feature and they're a small reminder of him every time I look in a mirror. But still, I was a constant reminder to him growing up of the woman that walked out. He loved me anyways and never once compared me to her, no matter what my crazy 13-year-old self thought. I know he wouldn't want me to have ill feelings toward her; he never once spoke badly about her. I'm just not interested in the woman that could do that to my Dad. The woman that could walk out on her only child and never look back.

Since he's been gone I've stuck mostly to work and the house. I still live in the house my Dad built for Rose. It's a little two bedroom cedar cabin that sets in the woods of southern Ohio. It may not seem like much with its tiny porch and dirt drive way, but to me it is heaven. I have no neighbors for at least a mile so I get the peace and quiet I crave, plus I can sit out on my porch swing in my pj's and not worry about anyone seeing me. Occasionally I get a visit from a wild animal trying to get into my strawberry patch (Dad and me started planting it when I was seven) and at least once a week one of Dad's old friends will come by to chat. They like to check up on me since he's been gone, though I've stopped answering the door when they come by.

I have no immediate family left since Dad died and as far as I know I don't have any distant family either. He was an only child (just like me), my Grandma died the same year I was born, and Pap passed away when I was 10. I don't know if I have any relatives left from Rose's side. Apparently the Aunt she lived with skipped town not long after she did and Dad had never met any other relatives though he said she spoke of family in Tennessee.

Feeling the sun pour through my window, I decide it's time to drag myself out of bed. I push the cover off me, climb out and head over to the closet. I grab my favorite pair of worn jeans and a simple white tank top then walk to the bathroom to take a shower. I'm determined not to spend the day in my pj's. I guess I ought a drag my behind into work while I'm at it so my boss Billy doesn't fire me. I haven't shown up for my shift in days, and I've been avoiding his calls and texts.

I hoped the warm water rolling over my skin would help to wash away some of my sadness, but no luck. I stayed in long enough that the water turned ice cold then climbed out to towel dry. Thankfully the mirror fogged over so I don't have to see my eyes while I brush my teeth. As much as I love them and the reminder of Dad, I'm already hanging on by a thread. I need to get through the day without crying. That's my new goal. I'm going to count the tearless days as small victories against the aching hole in my chest.

I contemplated fixing breakfast but settled for an apple. I doubt my stomach can handle much more, I'll probably get on a crying fit sometime in the day and it'll all come back up anyways. I speak out loud correcting myself, "No Bloom, stay positive. You will not cry today!"

Tossing the core in the trash I turn around, grab my keys and bag off the counter and head for the door. It's almost noon and the lunch rush should be starting. Billy will be so happy to have help that he might forgive me for not showing up the last several days.

As I step out of the house and off of the porch a summer breeze sweeps my hair to the side. It feels like a warm caress and I raise my face to the sun so I can fully feel the heat of the rays on my cheeks and the soft breeze on my skin. I let out a long soft sigh when I turn away from the light to head to the truck.

Chapter 2 – Pike

~ Strawberries & Cedar ~

Feeling the ground under my paws and the hot summer breeze in my coat as I run is the only thing I have to clear my head. I didn't think I'd run this far from home but I have a lot to clear out with killing my Dad and all. Don't get me wrong, I'm not the bad guy. I was just following pack law, but it doesn't change the fact that it's tearing me a part inside. Dad was always a strong man. The strongest in our pack, he over took the old alpha when he was 25 and had been leading us ever since, but he started to change when my mom died a year ago.

In our society she's what we would call his mate. A wolf shifter will do anything to love, care for, and protect their mate. I know what you're thinking but no, it's not what the humans have in their marriages, even when they refer to themselves as soul mates. In a true mating there is no risk of divorce, abuse, or even cheating. There's no such thing as a volatile mating. We physically can't harm our mates. Our wolf side is so protective he'd shred us apart from the inside if we even thought about causing them harm. From the moment we find our mate our life shifts and our mate becomes the center of our whole being. That's why when we lose our mate we don't usually last long after. It's as if half of our heart is ripped from us and we no longer wish to live. That's what a mate is, the other half of a shifter's heart, the part that anchors us to our humanity. Mom was the good part for Dad, and when she died all that was left was the hate and anger.

He started shirking his responsibilities. He wouldn't guide the new pups through their first change. He wasn't attending the pack meetings and started to revel in watching the wolves fight. As alpha he should've been stopping this mindless violence but he was drawn to the carnage. It all came to a head when he took the life of a pack elder who questioned him about his odd behavior. That's when the remaining pack elders came to me for help. I knew it was coming even though I tried to deny it. Pack law simply states that any pack member who becomes a lost wolf (a wolf who lets his dark side take control) will have to be "handled" by the pack Alpha, so they don't call attention to our kind. But in this case our Alpha was the lost wolf, and as his son it was my responsibility. I carry his alpha blood in my veins therefore I was the only one strong enough to take him down.

My mother died a year ago and now they wanted me to kill my father. I believed it's what he would've wanted; at least that's what I told myself. My father was nothing like this monster who was parading around in his body soiling his legacy. He would want to be at peace on the other side with his mate.

So six days ago I confronted him. It was a quick death. I took him down in less than five minutes while most of the pack watched. He didn't fight like an alpha is expected to. I think I even saw him smile when he drew his last breath. It was another sign he was ready to go. My sister, Emily, and I buried him beside our Mom in the local grave yard. He's finally at peace after a year of hell.

By taking Dad out I became the new pack alpha, a job I was not ready to assume. I had never wanted to be a leader and it was being forced upon me. So I did the only thing I could think to do and ran. I know it makes me sound like a coward and you should know I've never been one, but leading the pack of wolves who just demanded I kill part of my family wasn't something I could do yet. My wolf agreed with the decision to run, which should've been the first sign something big was about to happen. He's never backed down from a challenge, and leading the pack is undoubtedly a challenge. So I said bye to Emily and left word for my second-in-command, Tucker, to lead while I was gone. I've been running, in wolf form, ever since.

I've been across the Ohio line for several hours. This is the farthest I've ever run in my wolf form, and it's starting to feel a long way from my home in Tennessee. I haven't been in my human skin since the day we put Dad in the ground. I've been living off the rabbits my wolf hunted and bathing in the rivers and creeks I come across. A couple nights I've curled up under low hanging tree branches and tried to sleep, not that it ever comes. There's been too much running through my mind. My plan is to run until I'm too exhausted to think anymore then I'll let myself collapse and sleep for days. The exhaustion hasn't come. My damn wolf strength is keeping it at bay. I should've known it would mess up my plan.

Looking around the unfamiliar woods makes my wolf long for our home and pack. A wolf is always strongest when they're with their pack, and now that I was the alpha I seemed to draw more strength from them than ever. Even 500 miles from home I can still feel the ties that bind me to them and them to me. As much as it pained me to admit it, I missed them and I missed my sister. I hate worrying her; she'd been through enough losing both of our parents. She doesn't need to deal with a brother who's not man enough to face his responsibilities.

Curled up in a soft patch of grass under a large oak tree, I consider heading home. I can try to rest here a few hours then I'll turn around and go back to my responsibilities. I'm needed there and if I'm being honest I need them too. I was just laying my muzzle across my paws and closing my eyes when a shift of breeze brings a new scent to my nose. It hits me like a freight train and makes my ears prick up. It's such a simple mixture of smells, strawberries and cedar, but there's something else laced with it. The something else I know only I can smell and I know I have to find where it originates.

Screw rest!

I hop up and sprint full force through the trees again following the scent. I know with my wolf senses I can still be miles from my destination, but I don't care.

I'll run to the gates of hell and back if I can find who's creating that heavenly scent.

Chapter 3 – Bloom

~ A torture device used to open my freshly healing wounds ~

Pulling the truck into the parking spot I survey the lot to see if we're packed. It's the normal lunch rush from what I can tell. Taking a deep breath I silently remind myself I can handle this. Billy's Pizza Pub (his parents owned it before him and named the place after their only child) is one of the few restaurants in the small town near my home, but that doesn't matter even if the town was large it would still do well. The pizza is the best. Billy's sauce recipe was passed down to him from his great-great-grandmother or someone like that. So they had plenty of time to get it to perfection. He took over the restaurant when he was 20 and became a smash hit in this little town. Not that he was new to Jackson. He's lived here his entire life. In fact, he and my Dad had been best friends since kindergarten. That's why he gave me a job and I know that's why he hasn't fired me. But today's a new day and anything can happen, even that.

I work up the courage to walk in the door and I instantly hear Billy's voice coming from the kitchen. He catches sight of me as soon as he walks into the dining area and stops in his tracks. By the way he's looking at me, I can't tell if he's going to yell or scoop me up into a hug. He chooses the hug.

"Bloom, you've had me scared to death. Where have you been? Why haven't you been answering my calls or texts?" He rapidly shoots question after question my way.

He loosens the hug enough so he can look me over. He's checking for an injury. Of course there is none, well at least none he can see. I don't think he'll count the invisible hole I have in my chest. The concerned look he's giving me makes the guilt ten times worse when I softly say, "Sorry, I've been sleeping." Of course I've been crying more than sleeping, but he doesn't need to know that.

His mouth falls open in shock for a brief second then I see his expression turn from concern to anger. When he speaks I can tell he's trying to hold back his anger, "You mean I have been calling around checking on you all because you were sleeping. How the hell do you sleep for four days? I was on the verge of calling the police department to report you missing. I stopped by your house and you didn't answer. I about broke down the damn door just to make sure you weren't …" He stops himself right there, but I know what he was going to say. He thought I was dead. He glances over at the calendar that hangs by the register and then back at me before he scoops me back into the hug. "I'm sorry doll, I know you miss him. I can hardly believe it's been a year."

The anger I can handle but this I can't, not without crying. And crying is not an option! I gently wiggle out of his grip and say, "Billy, I'm sorry about the last several days. I shouldn't have left you shorthanded but as long as I still have a job I'd like to get to it."

Thankfully he can tell I'm not up to discussing what today is yet and says, "I'd never fire you doll. As long as you want a job you've got one here. Now get your butt to work." I'm so relieved I'm not going to be unemployed that I give him another hug before running into the back to grab my apron and order pad.

I've worked for Billy since I was sixteen. In this area jobs are hard to come by and most people have to drive 40 minutes to one of the bigger towns. So I was thrilled when he offered to let me work at the restaurant, even if it was only a couple days a week. After Dad was gone he knew I needed more money to keep up with the house bills so he upped my hours. Billy Garrison is just a big softy at heart, though he'll never admit it.

Several of my regular customers stop in during my shift, I think they heard I showed my face and want to make sure I'm alright. Billy's keeping an extra close eye on me as well. They're all waiting on me to fall to pieces, but I stay strong and don't shed a single tear. This is hard for me to accomplish, especially when someone grabs me into a big hug and whisper things they think are reassuring. The sweet words only make it harder to hold my tears inside. Part of me appreciates the thought but the other part of me sees the arms they're holding me in as a torture device used to open my freshly healing wounds.

On break I walk out back to get some air. Billy's is on the edge of town and the back borders the woods. I slide down the wall to sit on the cold ground and take a deep breath. I was only sitting there a few minutes when I hear the back door open and someone slide down beside me. I don't have to look over to know it's Billy. He lets out a sigh and then begins, "I was going to leave you be but after watching you today I think you need a reminder."

"A reminder?" What have I forgot? I've remembered every order I've taken tonight. Even with everything on my mind I haven't slipped up once. What do I need a reminder of?

"Of how much your Daddy loved you, Bloom."

"I know he did," is all I can manage to reply without crying. I can handle being lectured on messing up an order, heck I can even handle Billy firing me for not showing up. But this! I wasn't expecting this talk and I'm not ready for it either. But Billy isn't ready to give in and he gently takes my chin and turns me to face him.

"Bloom, he did and he wouldn't want to see you this way. You're so busy thinking about how he's gone that you're not remembering the good times you had when he was here. Heck you can't even bear to hear me tell you he loved you. I see the tears in your eyes doll." His calloused hand reaches out to wipe away a tear that breaks free from the boundary of my lids (darn him! I don't want to cry). "Your Daddy loving you isn't something to make you cry."

Closing my eyes I softly say, "I know Billy. I'm trying to heal."

"You're never going to fully heal doll, but you should be able to move on with your life. And I can tell you're not allowing yourself to do that. Have you even started cleaning out your Dad's room?"

"It's too soon!" I shout at him.

"I know it seems that way, but it might help." He ignores my outburst, thankfully.

"I don't think I can. I haven't even gone into his room since he's been gone."

"Would you like me to come do it for you?" he offers.

I know it's something I need to handle myself, "Billy I can't ask you to do that."

"You didn't ask, I offered. Your father was like my brother and that makes you my family. I'd do anything for my family Bloom and I can see you need this."

Giving in I flash him a faint smile and say, "Thanks, I think you're right. I need to start letting go."

"Just take it one day at a time doll. That's all any of us can do." With that Billy stands and offers his hand to help me up. I take it and he pulls me to my feet and into yet another hug. I'm seriously contemplating getting a t-shirt that reads "Stop Hugging Me!"

Letting me go he says, "I'll come over tomorrow morning before work and start if that's okay."

"Yeah that's fine."

"Good. Now let's get back in there. Your break's been over for about five minutes."

"I'll be right there if you don't mind."

He looks at me deciding whether or not he'll stay with me or go back in, but at that very second another waitress calls his name. "I'll be right there," looking back at me he tells me, "take your time. I'll cover your tables till you're back."

Once again I tell him thanks and then watch as he walks inside. Leaning back against the wall my gaze shifted back towards the woods. A dark shadow passes just inside the tree line. I can't make out anything other than it is huge. I start walking towards the woods. I don't know what the shadow is but I feel drawn in that direction. I'm a few feet away from the tree line when I hear my name called. Snapping out of it, I look around where I am and back into the woods before backing away quickly to go inside.

Chapter 4 – Pike

~ Seriously messing with my manly mind ~

I track the scent around 40 miles running between the tree line and corn fields. I'm lucky I'm not seen by someone dashing between the two. Normally I hide deep in the woods during the day. It's easier than being seen. People tend to be frightened by the size of my wolf. In my four-legged form I'm around 250 pounds and my head is still above most people's waist. I'm nearing a town and I can smell the restaurants and people, but I'm not looking for any of them. My nose veers me away from them and towards the woods. Ten minutes away I find where the scent is strongest, a small cedar cabin buried deep in the trees. The small porch has an old wooden swing hanging from its beams and there are green and white polka dotted curtains hanging in the window. Beside the front door there is a welcome sign carved with the family name Daniels. On the opposite edge of the yard I can smell a strawberry patch. It's late in the season but there still seems to be a few ripe berries that need to be picked. It's a modest home, but there's a charm. You can tell that the owner takes pride in the place. There are no vehicles in the driveway and I haven't picked up any sounds from inside the house so I decide to take a closer look.

Trotting up onto the front porch I glance into the large picture window. I see a nice size living room that opens up into a large kitchen. The living room is done in a rich brown with beautiful hardwood floors, and there are little touches of green from pillows on the couch to the rugs on the floor, even those polka dot curtains contained that same green. Along one wall sets two worn in brown leather recliners and a little side table. On the opposite wall is a flat screen with two bookshelves filled to the brim on either side, one containing books and the other DVDs. In front of the window there's a couch that matches the recliners. The hardwood floor flows into the kitchen but the walls in there are a buttery yellow instead of the brown and green. With my wolf sight I can make out the back door in the corner of the kitchen and I can see it's unlocked. Hmm, what kind of person doesn't lock their door? Must be my lucky day! Now I can take a closer look at the other rooms.

Leaping off the porch I hurry around back. Using my mouth I'm able to twist the door handle open without having to shift. That's a trick my father taught me as a kid and it's definitely come in handy since I started shifting. I wipe my paws on the mat by the door so I won't leave tracks then trot in. The scent is so strong it's like a punch in the gut. Taking a deep breath into my lungs, I let it fill and surround me. It makes me want to curl up right here on the kitchen floor and never leave. I shake my head trying to clear out the thought and walk further into the house. Crossing into the living room I stare at the bookshelf, it has an eclectic mix of biographies, psychology, fantasy, mysteries, and the classics. The person who lives here loves to read and their scent clings to every book. The DVD shelves are a different story. The scent marker on them is so faint you'd question if they've ever been handled. Beside the bookshelf is a hallway. The walls here are covered in photographs. There's a man holding a baby wrapped in a pink quilt in one. He's smiling down at the baby with such pride on his face but his eyes hold sadness. As I walk the hall I watch the girl grow from picture to picture. In one it's clearly her first day of school and she's clinging to her father's hand for dear life. A few pictures down she's a couple years older and she's standing next to a lake holding up a catfish grinning from ear to ear showing where she's missing her two front teeth. I'm enjoying watching her grow up in photographs from a kid to the awkward teen years and finally into a beautiful woman. From the picture that looks the most recent I'll guess she is in her early twenties. She's sitting between two men holding their hands in hers, one is clearly her father from the earlier photos (he still holds that sadness in his eyes) and the other is possibly an uncle though I don't see a resemblance. There are no photos of her and her mother. At that same end of the hall I reach her room. The walls are painted a pale blue and are bare except for the quote

"In dreams and in love there are no impossibilities" scrolled above her full size bed in black paint. The bed itself is unmade with the sheets and comforter twisted around each other at the end. On her night stand sets a worn copy of *The Notebook* and a pile of used tissues. I can smell the salty tears on them and begin to worry about her happiness. I blow out a breath at myself. I'm worrying about a woman I've never met, when she's crying over nothing more than a book. Her scent is making me crazy. In my 25 years I've never behaved this way about a woman.

Forcing myself out of her room I stroll to the next open door. It's a tiny bathroom with not much to see. The last door in the hall is closed so I use my handy little trick again. The room's musty from not being opened in awhile. The bed is made and there's a light layer of dust on the night stand. It's clearly a man's room, probably her fathers. I wonder where he is. He has more pictures on his dresser. One is a senior picture with the name Bloom printed in the bottom corner, such a fitting name for her. Bloom, Bloom

Daniels ... I let the name roll around in my head. I can't wait to shift back so I can feel how it rolls off my tongue. Strolling back out of the room I use my mouth to pull the door back closed, best to leave no sign someone's been here.

I take one more long deep breath to surround myself with her scent before walking out of her home. It's time to find Bloom. I feel I need to make sure she is alright. I pick up her scent again in the driveway and follow it back towards the town. Right at the edge of the woods, just inside the city limits, I come across a small brick building. I clearly smell tomato and pepperoni so it must be a pizza place. For being such a small building, the parking lot is packed. I keep to the tree line afraid of being seen and wait. I can tell she's in there. Her scent clings to the building. If I had clothes to change into I'd shift back to my human form and go in as a customer. But of course, there are no clothes around and I doubt the owner would appreciate a naked man strolling through his restaurant. That would break several health code violations. I chuckle in my mind thinking of how I want walk in there and sweep her off her feet. Emily's forced me to watch one too many "chick flicks" with her. Next time I see that sister of mine I'm letting her know her horrible choice in movies is seriously messing with my manly mind. From now on it's going to be action, horror, or none!

My ears prick up as a new sound comes to me. It's as gentle as the breeze and seems to stroke my mind. It takes me a moment to realize I'm hearing her thoughts. I close my eyes to enjoy the feeling of her thoughts inside my head.

You will not cry! You will not cry! You will <u>NOT</u> cry! Geez will these people stop trying to console me. Can't they see they're only making this harder? I think it's time for me to take my break. Ugh! I need some fresh air and less people around.

Her sadness hits me as soon as she walks out the back door. It's hard enough to hear her worrying in her head but now I actually feel it creeping up into my fur. The feeling makes my wolf restless and I have to stop him from running over to console her. Thankfully a middle-aged man comes out to speak with her and that helps to distract my wolf enough that I can hold back the urge to run to her.

Hanging on to every word of their conversation, I find out she's lost her father too. It causes my heart to ache for my father and for the pain of her losing hers. It's odd how I'm feeling her emotions as if they're mine. I've never met her father and I want to cry at the loss of him. When I watch this man, Billy, place his hand on her face I have to hold back my growl. I can tell he means her no harm, but my wolf's angry at the man for touching her. He itches to be the one comforting her.

I listen as he tries to sooth her and become very grateful towards the man when he offers to help clear out her Dad's belongings. This Billy guy is family to her which makes him family to me. So no more growling at him and I'll have to find a way to repay him for helping my Bloom when I couldn't. My Bloom, I like the sound of that.

He stands up, kindly helps her to her feet, and then he's called back inside. She leans against the building staring at the woods and I long to be closer to her so I take the chance and move towards the thinning tree line. I see it in her eyes when she catches sight of me. As much as I want to reveal myself to her, my wolf knows we need to hold off a little longer, so I dash back into the shadows before she has the chance to register what she's seen. I listen to her thoughts.

That is huge. What can it be?

I watch as she involuntarily moves closer towards the trees. She's drawn to me just as I am to her. Good to see this isn't one sided.

Someone hollers her name and she snaps out of her daze. She looks at the door of the restaurant and back into the woods. She's scared herself, that's easy to see as she practically runs back inside to get away from what the shadows hold.

Laying in the tree line I keep my eyes locked on the pizza place. The light fades away and the night swoops in but I can't take my eyes away. Finally when all the customers have left she walks back outside surrounded by a group of her co-workers. They invite her out to the local bar but she declines. With a wave and a slight smile she says goodbye and climbs into a large truck and pulls out.

I could easily track her scent to follow where she's going but there is no need for that because now I can read her thoughts. And the only thing on her mind is home.

Chapter 5 – Bloom

~ I'm not sure what I'm going to do without you ~

Walking into the house I kick my shoes off by the door and toss my keys at the counter. By the end of the night I felt like my shift would never end, but thankfully it did. Some of the other waitresses invited me to go to Hudson's bar but I declined. The only thing I wanted to do is get home and take a long bath. I had a shower this morning, but after working I smell like pepperoni and I need the water to relax away the painful memories today brought up.

I run the water and dump in some strawberry bath beads. I'm not a person who likes to smell like flowers or even vanilla but I love the smell of strawberries. I test the water with my toe; it's warm but not scolding hot, so I plop the rest of my body into the water. After thoroughly washing the pepperoni smell out of my hair and off of my skin I close my eyes laying my head back to enjoy the feeling of the water relaxing my muscles. I fell asleep that way.

The sound of a text message coming through my phone wakes me up. The water has already chilled so I pull the plug and climb out. I dry myself and grab the phone off the bathroom sink The text message is from Billy.

Just a reminder I'll be there in the morning. Sleep tight!

I send back a quick response.

K I'll see you then. Night!

By the time on my phone I have napped for almost an hour. I know I won't be able to get back to sleep right away so I get dressed, grab a bottle of water out of the fridge and head outside. I momentarily flick on the porch light but think twice and flick it back off. The sky is clear and even though the moon isn't full I can see clearly. I climb onto to the old porch swing and lay with my face down on the cushions. Using my hands I push till I have a nice slow swinging motion then I tuck both arms under my head and look out at the night sky.

Watching the stars remind me of Dad and before I know it I'm talking out loud to him, confessing things I never got the chance to. "I love Rose's cross necklace you gave me. I'm sorry I had been such a brat when I found out it was hers. I'm also sorry she left I know you loved her, and I'm sorry I don't." I let that thought linger in the quiet night before I continue, "Oh, remember when those two bottles of beer came up missing when I was 14. Well it was me and Bonnie. We thought it would make us cool sneaking and drinking them. We learned our lesson though, we were sick the whole next day."

"Billy's been good to me since you've been gone. Not that you didn't already know he would. He misses you …" the tears start, "and Daddy I miss you too. So much!" Tears are now falling freely from my eyes as I choke out my last confession of the night, "I'm not sure what I'm going to do without you." I curl around myself as the sobs rock my body.

Chapter 6 – Pike

~ Caught in her trap ~

I've been sitting at the edge of the woods near the strawberry patch listening to her. But when the tears start my wolf's need to protect her, even from her own sorrow, is so great that I lose control and start running from my hiding spot. I don't even make it out of the trees when I feel the cold hard metal latch onto my front paw. I howl in pain. If she didn't know I was close before she definitely does now and I can't get this damn trap off even if I do shift. Crap!

Chapter 7 – Bloom

~ Come with me ~

The sound of a dog howling in pain snaps me out of the crying. It sounds like he's over near the woods. Oh crap! He probably got caught in one of the old animal traps Dad put out to keep the coons out of my strawberries. Wiping my eyes, I scramble to my feet and run inside to grab a flash light. He sounds like he's in pain and I can't leave him like that. Pointing the beam from the light into the woods I take a breath to steady my nerves then walk in. I find him lying on his side, I was right he has his foot in one of those old traps. I don't walk over to him right away I can't. He's huge! I've seen large dogs, my friend Bonnie use to have a Saint Bernard and he was large, but he looks like a pup compared to this dog. I'd say he's a wolf but I know wolves don't get this large. He could be a mixed breed. His coat is so ... black. Not a dull black either, jet black and when the moon shines on him, the tips look blue. When my eyes finally find his

I notice they're locked on me. They're the most striking blue, like staring into the clearest blue ocean. I can't look away from him. If I do I feel I'll lose something, though I'm not sure what. Then he whimpers and my eyes fly to his paw still in the trap. I close the distance and fall to my knees. Using all my strength I pry the trap open. He doesn't move just sits there and watches me but when the trap is finally off he tries to stand.

He's favoring that leg and I can see the wound is deep. He needs it cleaned up and bandaged, but how do I explain that to a 300 lb dog? Standing up I hold my hand out. I want to touch his coat but I feel I need his permission. He watches my face then glances at my hand. Limping closer he rubs his muzzle across my palm. Thank goodness he's friendly. It might make it easier to get him inside. Walking back towards the house I pat my leg and in a soothing voice call, "Come on boy. Come with me. It's okay. I just need to clean your paw." To my surprise he follows me all the way into the house without a problem.

I grab the first aid kit from under the kitchen sink and a bowl of warm water, and then I get started on cleaning the wound. It's deep and probably needs stitches but the vet won't be open till tomorrow so this will have to do till then. For a dog he is rather attentive. He watches everything I do for him. His eyes never leave me and he doesn't try to pull away.

Closing the first aid kit and wiping off my hands I look at him. He really is gorgeous, huge, but gorgeous. And he must belong to someone because he looks well taken care of. I've never seen a stray that looks this good. Running my hands down his side I ask, "So boy what's your name and why are you all the way out here?"

Chapter 8 – Pike

~ Please, don't call me Rover ~

I'm screaming in my head. ***Pike. My name is Pike! Please don't call me Rover or some ridiculous dog name like that.*** Geez I hope she can hear me like I can her. She's so beautiful maybe I should shift right now and take her in my arms. Damn it Pike think straight. You don't want to scare her to death. I can't think with her hand rubbing down my side like this. This woman is going to be my down fall.

Chapter 9 – Bloom

~ You got a dog? ~

The name comes to me like it's sent from somewhere else. But looking at him it seems right so I test it, "Pike! Is your name Pike boy?" His ears prick and at the time I'd swear he actually nods his head yes (but it's late and I'm sleepy so I could be seeing things). "Okay Pike it is," I say around a yawn then add, "Well Pike, I better make you a bed so we both can get some rest." I stand to walk to the bedroom and he follows me. I dig a couple old comforters out of my closet and make a spot for him in the kitchen next to a bowl of water. He sniffs at the blankets then looks at me. Yawning, "Sorry boy, best I can do. I'm going to bed. Now get some sleep."

I watch him as he curls up in the comforters then I head to the bathroom to brush my teeth. Watching myself in the mirror I notice the dark circles that have been staying under my eyes are gone and even after working all day I look refreshed. Hmm! Must be that nap I took in the bath earlier.

I crawl in between my covers and I'm prepared to fall asleep when I feel the movement on the bed. Pike has jumped in beside me and is making himself comfortable. He lays his head across the pillow next to me and his blue eyes lock on mine. I don't have the energy to kick him out, at least that's what I tell myself. So I throw my arm around him, rubbing my fingers through his soft coat. He licks my nose making me giggle. It's been awhile since I've heard that sound come out of my mouth. Moving my hand up to rub his muzzle I tell him, "Thanks boy I needed that. And you can stay with me tonight but tomorrow you're back in the kitchen. I don't want my bed smelling like dog." Not that he smells like a normal dog. He actually smells like the forest after a rain storm has washed it clean.

For the first time in a year I sleep without tossing and turning, without the dreams of Dad crashing. I'm out until the warm sun peeking through my curtains forces my eyes open. Pike is still stretched out beside me with his head on the pillow and my arm around him. We haven't moved an inch. Stretching my arms over my head I sit up and look at the clock, 9 a.m. Good, I'll be ready before Billy gets here. Rubbing Pike behind the ears I whisper, "Come on boy it's time to start our day. How about I fix us some breakfast?"

His eyes fly open at the mention of food and he licks my face. Gently pushing him back down and wiping off my cheek. "I'm not sure I can get use to these dog kisses. Geez, you need a mint Pike."

He hangs his head like his feelings are hurt and I feel horrible. I'm not sure if he understands what I said or why I feel the need to comfort him, but I do. Grabbing his muzzle in my hands I turn him to face me, putting my nose to his. "I was kidding Pike. You can give me doggie kisses anytime. But if you're going to be here awhile we will be getting you a doggie tooth brush."

Letting go of his face and hopping out of bed I look back at him. "Okay now let's get some food. I'm starving." He follows my lead and leaps out too, then follows me into the kitchen.

I've never had a dog before so there isn't any dog food in the house, and I'm not sure what dogs can and cannot eat. So looking in the fridge I dial my friend Bonnie. Her Dad's a vet and she has a dog so she'll know. I hear the line pick up and then her cheerful voice, "Hey Beautiful! I haven't heard from you in awhile."

Her warmth always makes me smile. She's been my best friend since the third grade when she skipped (yes she skipped then and occasionally still does) over and asked me to play My Little Ponies with her. It's been Bonnie & Bloom ever since. I like to say she brings the sun when it's been cloudy. That's why I've been avoiding her. I'm not ready for the sun. *"Hey Bon!"*

"Hey, I've missed you girl." I can hear the relief in her voice that hearing from me brings.

"I've missed you too, Bon. I've called because I've got a question for ya."

"Hit me with it."

"What do dogs eat other than dog food?"

"You got a dog?"

"No … well kind of temporarily. He got caught in one of Dad's old coon traps last night and I brought him in to clean his wounds and I let him stay with me. I thought I'd bring him in to your Dad's office today so he can check out his paw."

"That was sweet of ya. I'm sure Dad will be glad to check him over. So are you keeping him? It might be good for you to have a pet with ya out there to keep ya company."

"I'm not sure. He probably has a family looking for him. So what can I feed Pike?"

"Pike? Did you name him or did he have a dog tag?"

"No tags. I just didn't want to call him dog or boy and Pike seems to fit. He responds to it so he must like the name. So what kind of food is okay?" Bonnie is sweet but her thoughts wander a bit, hence having to ask the same question three times before getting an answer.

"If you have some leftover chicken he'll probably eat that. They also like apples and peanut butter. But if you're coming to Dad's office you should pick up a bag of dog food. You don't want him getting use to table scraps."

Grabbing a bowl of leftover chicken from the fridge I tell her, "I'll do that. Thanks Bon."

"Anytime Blu. Do you want to meet up at Dads and have lunch while he's checking out your dog?" I can tell she's nervous I'll turn her down. I've been doing that to everyone lately, but today feels like the perfect day to see my best friend.

"That sounds great. What time do you want to meet?"

"How does noon sound? I'll stop and pick-up a couple burgers." Bonnie's so happy, all because I've agreed to see her. She'll probably have a joker sized smile plastered to her face all day. I can even see her jumping up and down, doing her victory dance.

"Sounds perfect to me. Don't forget the fries and grab a burger for Pike too, please." I bite my lip to keep myself from laughing at the image of Bonnie doing her victory dance.

"I can do that."

"Bon?"

"Yeah?"

"I'm sorry I've been M.I.A." I hate bringing down the good mood we've had going on, but I owe my friend an apology.

"Blu, you have nothing to be sorry about. I knew you'd call when you were ready. Love ya chickadee." I can hear the tremble in her voice.

"Love you too." I end the call before we both end up bawling.

"How does chicken sound?" I ask turning my attention back to Pike.

I warm up his leftover chicken and then make myself some scrambled eggs and toast. Pike devours his leftovers before the toast pops up, so I give him a slice of it as well. I'm nibbling on mine when I hear the knock on the door. I have to calm Pike who becomes very alert and then I head to the door to let Billy inside. Pike follows me, or should I say leads the way. He must have been trained as a guard dog because he growls at Billy until I reassure him he's safe.

Stepping inside Billy asks, "When did you get a dog? Or should I say horse, that beast is huge."

"Found him caught in one of Dad's old coon traps last night. He is pretty large isn't he? No need to worry though he's like a big cuddly teddy bear."

"By the way he was just growling at me I wouldn't say he's too cuddly. But I do think it's a good idea for you to have a dog. He'll keep you company and seems like a good guard too."

"I've lived here all my life and no-one has messed with this place. Plus, I never said I'm keeping him. Like I told Bonnie he probably has a family looking for him. I should probably hang up some flyers or post his picture on my Facebook. Maybe someone will recognize him."

"Just because no-one has doesn't mean they won't. If the wrong person realizes it's just you out here they might try something. Don't let your guard down doll. But I think you should keep the dog." He watches Pike who is pressed against my leg with his gaze locked on Billy. "He's taken to you quick."

"I won't let my guard down and you know I have Dad's old hand gun if some fool does try something," I remind him.

"Good to hear. Just make sure you remember to take the safety off. It doesn't shoot when it's on," he says with a grin. Billy knows I'm a great shot, he and Dad taught me to shoot when I was a kid, but that doesn't change the fact that he likes to tease me.

"Oh give me a break old man. I'm a better shot than you." I push his shoulder teasingly.

"Well you did learn from the best. This old man is hungry. Do you have any breakfast left?" he asks rubbing his shoulder, as if I could really hurt him.

Heading towards the kitchen I call, "come on I'll find you something to eat."

I whip him up some scrambled eggs and toast and then sit at the table with him drinking my apple juice. Pike is once again curled up beside my feet and I'm rubbing my toes through the fur on his side. Billy's not normally a quiet man but when you put food in front of him you get quiet time. Though it doesn't take him long to finish because the man doesn't eat, he inhales his food. Sitting his fork down and wiping his mouth he asks, "So are you ready for me to start doll?"

"Are you ready?" I ask back.

"You know what I'm talking about Bloom Michael." You can always tell an adult is being serious when they use your first and middle name.

"I'm ready Billy, but if you don't mind I won't be helping. I'm not sure I can go through his stuff yet." I admit, not meeting his eyes because apparently watching the condensation on my glass is more important.

He places his hand under my chin, forcing me to look him in the eyes. "I know doll, that's why I'm here." He stands up from the table, comes around Pike and gives me a one armed hug. "I'm going to get started. Holler if you need me to save you from that bear of a dog."

"Not needed Billy. He's a teddy bear." I prove it by getting on the floor with Pike and cuddling him close to my chest.

"Yeah yeah a 300 lb teddy bear that can rip out a man's throat. Real cuddly," I hear him mumble as he walks out of the kitchen.

After cleaning up the mess from breakfast I decide to straighten up the living room as well. I'm elbow deep in the dust bunnies behind the couch when I feel Pike nudging my leg. Crawling out and wiping my hands on my jeans I ask him, "What's wrong?"

He turns and points his head towards the clock hanging on the wall. I have less than thirty minutes to get ready and drive to town to meet Bonnie. How a dog can know that is baffling, but I have no time to think about it because I have to get ready. Hopping up I rush into the bathroom and start stripping off my dirt covered clothes and take the quickest shower of my life. In my haste I forget clean clothes, which normally wouldn't be a problem but with Billy in the house I can't walk around in a towel, so I peek out the door to see if the coast is clear then begin a mad dash for my room. I make it all of two steps before I trip and fall over Pike who has decided to stand guard at the bathroom door. Trying to grasp the wall to stop my fall I manage to pull a couple picture frames down with me. I'm trying to stand up, hoping Billy didn't hear my fall, but no such luck because he comes running out of Dad's room.

"Are you okay doll?" He asks stopping just short of the broken frames.

Pulling the towel around me tighter and trying to maneuver around the glass shards, "I'm fine. I just tripped."

"You look like you started a fight with the wall of pictures and the pictures won. And your knee's a little banged up. Do you want me to check it out? You might have glass in the cut." He makes a move to come help me but Pike instantly gets in his way. Billy tries to move to the other side to get by but Pike's faster and blocks that way as well.

The two stare each other down for a good minute, before Billy looks away. Pike must have won because Billy throws his hands up, "Fine pup I won't doctor up her knee. Sorry doll it looks like your guard refuses to let me help you. You best go clean up that knee before you bleed all over the floor. I'll get the broom and clean this glass up." Then he proceeds to stomp toward the kitchen.

Running my hand through Pike's coat in a soothing voice I tell him, "Okay come with me you big brute. I'll clean up my own knee. No help from Billy."

Yelling after Billy's retreating form, "Sorry, I'm not sure why he's acting this way. Thanks for getting the glass though."

"No problem. Just don't let that horse boss you around, if you start now he'll always have the upper hand." Billy calls from the kitchen.

Heading back to the bathroom I holler over my shoulder, "He's just a dog Billy. He can't boss anyone around."

"Tell that to him!" I hear him reply in a chuckle.

Chapter 10 – Pike

~ I'm a little taken with him as well ~

Take out the part where the trap caught my paw and last night was one of the best nights of my life. It took all the control I have not to shift back to my human form while I was laying in bed with her. God, if she knew what was racing through my mind when she was rubbing her hands over my coat she'd stop thinking of me as an innocent dog.

A dog! The woman thinks I'm a dog, and not even a scary dog. A dog she trusted enough to bring into her home and allows to share her bed.

I've been called a lot of things over the years, including being likened to a hell hound, come to bring the wrath of Satan, but nobody has ever mistaken me for a common house pet. I can't decide if I'm insulted or should be happy that I don't scare her. Okay, I am happy she's not afraid of me, but I think my alpha ego is bruised. I'm supposed to intimidate people. People like Billy, but you see how that's going. And I know I promised no more growling at this guy, but I can't help myself when she's running around in those tiny shorts she tries to pass off as pajamas.

Hell, because of the little towel move she just pulled I almost killed the man. She would've never forgiven me for that one; I don't care how nice of a guy he may be, he's rubbing my wolf and me the wrong way. My wolf doesn't want anyone but him around her when she's practically naked. What the heck happened to flannel pajamas or even a robe? It would've been a much more sensible choice when you have a man running around your home that's not your mate. If it's just her and me she could lose the towel and I'd be fine, more than fine. I'd shift and have her in my arms in less than a heartbeat. But no, she has to run around in baby doll sized shorts and towels that are meant to clean dishes not cover wet bodies. This woman is so going to be the death of me, a beautiful death, but a death none the less.

Then there's Billy. I'm not sure what it is about this man, but he seems to know more than he's letting on. Ever since he tried to stare me down in the hallway I've been expecting him to out me as a shifter. I know there are humans that know the truth about us, hell most of the humans in our small town know that we exist and they protect the secret. But I've seen no sign of shifter activity in this community so how can this man know. I just hope the old fool doesn't out me before I have to chance to do it myself. She needs to hear it from me, not him.

Reminding her of the time was a huge mistake on my part, but thankfully she was too preoccupied to analyze that she was reminded by her "dog." I'll have to be extra careful around her or she's going to figure out herself that I'm not an ordinary canine.

I watch her clean up her knee, which is unbelievably hard. I've never wanted to care for someone who isn't my family, and with her I'm becoming annoyingly protective. Once she has it bandaged up I rub my muzzle against her hand, it seems to reassure me in a way I never believed possible. Her touch has a soothing affect on my wolf, I'm not sure if it's a mate thing or Bloom thing. I'm leaning more towards it being a Bloom thing.

It takes her less than five minutes to finish getting ready. I expected her to get dolled up, most of the women I know won't leave the house without a couple layers of make-up and their hair poufed to perfection, but like I said she keeps surprising me. She braids her wet hair and throws on a pair of worn Levi's and a lace trimmed tank and absolutely no make-up touches her face. She leaves me with no other choice but to openly drink her in with my eyes. Though to her it probably looked like a normal dog with his tongue hanging out. I've always been comfortable as my wolf but there's something about Bloom that has me craving my two legged form more.

Following her to the truck I wait as she opens the door for me then leap into the passenger seat. She climbs into the driver's side and heads us toward town. We're running late so she calls her friend and lets her know we're on our way. The woman drives like she is in the Indy 500, taking curves on two wheels. I can't look out the windows without it making me car sick and the thought of sticking my big wolf head out the window for air is even scarier. She'll probably take my head off with a mail box if I do. Giving up on watching the road I lay my head on her lap. She takes one hand off the wheel to rub behind my ears the rest of the way to town, which both pleases and scares me. The thought of her driving this reckless with only one hand is extremely frightening, but I can't force myself to move away from her touch. So if we die in a fiery crash, so be it, at least I can say I have her hands on me when I go.

Less than 15 minutes after leaving the house I feel the truck come to a stop and she shifts into park. We exit the truck and walk towards a brick building that's situated next to a small park. A little bell jingles against the door when we walk in and looking around I take in all the pet supplies. I'm letting this woman bring me to a freaking Vet. She'll owe me big time for this one. I know my paw has already healed thanks to my shifter DNA, but she doesn't know that so I should be thankful she cares enough to get me treatment.

Sitting behind the receptionist desk is a girl about the same age as Bloom. She has hair the color of milk chocolate pulled into a loose bun and a smile that could rival the sun in brightness. When she notices Bloom she jumps from her seat and bounces across the room to pull her into a hug. Bloom hugs her back with the same amount of enthusiasm; this must be the girl from the phone. I've never been great with names. Was it Betsy, Billy, I'm pretty sure it starts with a B.

Turning towards me Bloom answers the question on my mind, "Bonnie this is Pike. Pike this is Bonnie. Her Dad's going to check out your paw."

Bonnie crouches down in front of me and rubs her hands through my coat, "Geez he's huge Blu. Are you sure he isn't part horse?"

"Billy keeps referring to him as a bear, but I'm leaning towards part wolf." Blooms eyes zone in on Bonnie's hands and I can tell she's forcing herself to act like it's no big deal.

"Wolf? He's much too large to be a wolf breed. Well at least all the hybrid wolf breeds I've seen come through here. Maybe Dad can give you an idea. He is gorgeous whatever mix he may be. I don't think I've ever seen a black coat this vibrant and those blue eyes." Bonnie lets out a whistle.

I do my best to stay still and unthreatening as she inspects me. Though my wolf wants her hands off of him, hers aren't made to touch him. I again look at my unaware mate and see the same struggle going through her. She loves her friend but she can't stand to see someone else's hands on me, but she's fighting the urge to push her friend away and claim me as hers. She doesn't understand why she's so possessive over me, but I love hearing those thoughts coming from her beautiful mind.

Grabbing Bonnie's attention back from me she asks, "So is your Dad available?"

"Oh, yeah! He said to bring you right back. I think he's excited to see ya." Bonnie finally takes her hands off of me and stands up.

Just then a plump man with snow white hair and rosy cheeks walks into the room. If he grows a beard he could easily pass for Santa. "Of course I'm excited to see my other favorite girl." He pulls Bloom into a big hug, "It's been too long."

"I've missed you too Mr. Harris. Thanks for agreeing to check out Pike's paw." She hugs him then puts space between them.

Mr. Harris turns his attention to me. "Anything for one of my girls. Bring this big guy back into my exam room."

I follow the two of them into a tiny white room and plop down next to Bloom's feet. Mr. Harris snaps on a pair of exam gloves then he turns that million dollar smile to us. "Bloom, why don't you go ahead and have that lunch with Bonnie. I'll fix Pike up then I'll bring him out to join you two."

"Okay, but Mr. Harris first can you tell me what breed is Pike?"

He looks me over quickly then shoots back, "He's definitely a wolf hybrid and by his size he has to have a giant dog breed in him. Wolves alone don't get anywhere near this size. He might be part Mastiff. I can't say for sure. Has he shown any aggression?"

"He got a little funny when Billy was around, but I wouldn't say he was aggressive. He seems more protective. I'm thinking maybe he was someone's guard dog. Do you recognize him at all?"

"No, he's not a patient of mine. He could've been trained to be a guard dog; he's definitely big enough for the task. He seems taken with you."

Scratching behind my ears she confesses, "To be honest I'm a little taken with him as well."

Mr. Harris doesn't respond, he just gives her a knowing smile and changes the subject, "Well your lunch is probably getting cold. Go join Bonnie and when I'm done I'll bring him back to you."

She bends down and kisses the top of my head and whispers just loud enough for me to hear, "Mr. Harris is a nice man and he'll take good care of you so listen to what he has to say. I'll be right outside waiting on you." Then standing back up, "Thanks for checking him out Mr. Harris."

"You're welcome Bloom. Now get to your lunch so I can get started."

She gives us both one last smile then exits the room. Mr. Harris turns back to me and starts un-wrapping the bandage Bloom put on my paw the night before. The wound's almost healed, but that doesn't seem to shock him. He cleans the area and puts on an ointment. Taking off his gloves and throwing them in the trash he crosses over to the door and slides the lock into place. He turns back to me with his arms crossed over his chest and the kindness that had been there before gone and demands, "Shift now!"

Chapter 11 – Pike

~ That's not my story to tell ~

I'm so shocked I just stare at the man for a good five minutes before I let the change take me. He watches as it slides over my body and the fur recedes back into my skin, but it doesn't faze him. You'd think it was normal for him to see one of his animal patients change into a human, hell maybe it is. After the last few days I'd say anything's possible.

My voice's rough from not talking for so long but I manage to grumble, "How do you know?"

He uncrosses his arms and pulls the small doctors stool over and explains, "We had a shifter who lived here years ago. She taught me a little about your kind. Why are you here?"

I look the man over and feel he's telling the truth, but he doesn't need my full story, yet. I cross over to the little sink in the room and grab a mug that's sitting on the counter and fill it with cold water. Once I down the whole mug I answer, "I needed to get away from my pack for awhile and seemed drawn here."

"How's the pack dealing without their alpha?"

That female wolf spilled an awful lot it seems, "Yes I'm the alpha. I haven't been one long and the last time I checked they're doing fine. Why did this female wolf tell you so much about our kind?"

"That's not my story to tell so I'll just say we *were* friends." As in they no longer are. Hmm, interesting.

"Who can tell me the story?"

"Why do you need to know?"

Good question. Why do I want to know about this female? It's not against our laws to tell people about us, as long as they can be trusted. I decide to be honest. "I'm not sure. But I feel it might be important."

He looks me over searching for whether I can be trusted and then coming to his decision he nods his head and says, "Billy may tell you the story. If he feels you need to know. But before we decide whether to tell you, we need to know what your intentions are with Bloom." Why the heck aren't the people in this town intimidated by me? I'm the alpha for goodness sakes. No one from back home would ever question me or any other alphas this way.

"With respect sir, I think she needs to hear what my intentions are before I tell you."

"You think she's your mate!" How a man with such a kind face can sound so hateful I don't know, but he pulls it off.

Staring him down I reply through gritted teeth, "I don't think. I know she's my mate. I imagine that friend of yours told you how a mating works."

"She said a little."

"Well let me inform you of this little fact about a mating." I make sure to emphasize my words putting a little of my alpha authority in them, "You *do not* try to come between a wolf and his mate!"

He scoots his stool closer to the door and holds his hands up in surrender, "Calm down I'm not trying to come between you and your mate. I just have to make sure Bloom doesn't get hurt anymore."

"I can respect that, but you have to realize I'd give my life to protect her."

"When are you going to tell her?"

Releasing the alpha tone from my voice I let out a sigh, "I don't know. Have any advice?"

"Yeah, tell her before Billy does. He has a hard time keeping secrets, especially one this good." Then his face softens and the love he has for my mate shows clearly. "Bloom really is like my other daughter Pike and I want to see her happy. So I hope she takes hearing the truth from you well."

"I hope she does too." She's already connecting with me threw the bond, even though she doesn't understand it yet. Once she knows the truth it won't be too hard to convince her shifters exist and that we belong to each other. At least I'm hoping.

"Well you best shift back so I can take you back to her, unless you want to fess up now."

"I think she needs to see the shift for herself and I'm not sure she's ready for that. So I'll wait."

"You're probably right. But give her some credit she's handled a lot over the years and I believe she'll handle this just as well."

A response isn't needed so I nod and start the shift back to my wolf form. Mr. Harris leads me out of the room and through the lobby. The girls aren't there so he tells me they've probably taken their lunch to the park next door. He flips the sign to closed and guides me to what he says is their favorite spot. I don't need him to guide me to her, I can find her by following her scent but people might take notice of a huge "dog" wandering around by himself.

Her favorite spot's on the opposite side of the park. A stone picnic table that sets in the sun by a small creek that runs along the back side of the grounds. She's sitting on top of the table with her back to us and her face lifted to the sun. Bonnie's rambling on about some party at a lake and Bloom's politely listening but from her thoughts I know she isn't interested in the slightest. The lake holds a lot of memories of her

Dad and as much as she likes to spend time with Bonnie and some of her other friends she's not sure she's ready.

I stop to admire her sitting there while Mr. Harris walks the rest of the way over. He makes himself known by grabbing one of his daughter's fries and sitting down next to her. At his arrival Bloom sits up and looks for me. When she finds me still standing several feet away she hops off of the table and jogs over throwing her arms around me for a hug. She rubs my side and then looks at my un-bandaged un-injured paw and with her brows stitched together asks Mr. Harris, "His paw's already healed?"

Swallowing the fry that's in his mouth, "Yeah, you did a really good job treating the area last night."

"I could've sworn he'd need some stitches." She continues eyeing my newly healed paw.

"It was late last night when it happened right? It probably just seemed worse because you were so tired." Mr. Harris tries to cover.

She looks over at him and back at me like she's missing something. "Maybe you're right. It was kind of late." I can tell she doesn't buy the answer, she just doesn't want to seem ungrateful for him checking me out and she's not sure why he'd lie to her so she drops the subject.

Chapter 12 – Bloom

~ Going on with my life ~

I'm trying to listen to Bonnie talk about the party at the lake while I feed Pike his sandwich, but I can't stop wondering how Pike's paw healed so fast and why Mr. Harris acts like it's no big deal. I may have been numb to the world this last year but that doesn't mean I lost my mind. What makes my suspicions worse is that this man who's been like my second father keeps glancing between Pike and myself like he's waiting for one of us to pull a gun on him.

"So are you going to come to the party Blu?" Bonnie asks pulling my attention back to her.

"Sure. When's it again?"

"Thursday and don't forget to bring a couple of poles. We can try to catch a few fish while we're there," she says clearly trying to suppress a squeal of delight about my agreeing to come.

"I can cover that."

"Everyone'll be so excited to see you. I know some of the guys will be there. They might even throw together a bonfire. It'll be just like the old days Blu. You'll see!"

I don't have the heart to tell her in the old days we would've tried to sneak past my Dad so we wouldn't get caught coming in past curfew, and Dad's no longer alive to catch us. But I don't want to bring down her happiness. So far today's been a good day. The hole in my chest is still there, I feel the pain of missing him, but the hole seems to be getting smaller. I doubt it'll ever completely heal because I'll always miss him, but it'll heal enough that I'll be able to go on with my life like he would've wanted.

Bonnie realizes I've stopped listening to her once again because she stops talking and proceeds to gather up our mess from lunch. Mr. Harris's already left; he must have grown tired of giving me cryptic glances and listening to Bonnie rattle on about the party. Pike who's now full from eating his sandwich, mine, and part of Bonnie's is curled up by my feet looking rather content. I stand and give Bonnie a hug bye with the promise I'll see her Thursday then Pike and I head home.

Billy's coming out of the house, his arms filled with boxes when we pull in. Sliding out of the truck and holding the door open for Pike to follow I holler, "Do you need me to grab one of those for you?"

Peeking his head around the side of one, "I can handle this. I'm just taking some things out to the shed."

I watch him maneuver down the porch steps then concede, "Okay, but if you change your mind let me know."

"I will."

I begin to head inside but turn back to look for Pike when I realize he's still at the bottom of the steps watching Billy. Billy notices too, "He probably needs to stretch his legs after the ride back from town. Why don't you let him stay out here with me for awhile?"

"Okay but if he gets in the way just bring him back into me. I'm going to go start some laundry."

"Okay, Blu." Billy agrees then turning to Pike says, "Come on pup before I drop these boxes."

I watch as they walk around the edge of the house then I head inside.

Chapter 13 – Pike

~ Rose's Story ~

I follow Billy to the back of the property where a small shed sets at the tree line. I listen for the front door closing to signal Bloom making it inside and expect him to start talking as soon as we're out of hearing range, but he says nothing. He sets the boxes down just inside the door of the shed then opens the top one and pulls out a small album. I watch him as he takes a seat next to the pile of boxes and looks through the tiny black book. There's the shadow of a smile across his face but it never reaches his eyes. I want to shift so I can talk to him but I have the feeling he'll spill more if I stay in this form. So I set there watching him re-live whatever's in that album.

Finally, when he reaches the last page he looks at me and nods. He's going to tell me the story of the she-wolf and he needs me to listen. He doesn't say it but I see it in his eyes how important this story is to him. I don't realize how much it's going to affect me to till he turns the album to face me and sets it on the ground open to the last page. There staring back at me is a face I've become all too familiar with since childhood, one that's been in my life just as much as my own parents if not more. And she's holding a newborn version of Bloom. I keep shifting between the woman and child waiting for reality to sink in. The resemblance should've been obvious the moment I saw her but I've been so caught up in finding my mate that it didn't sink in. But now it's so obvious I can't deny it even if I want to. Bloom's the daughter of a shifter!

Billy waits until the realization shows in my eyes then he begins, "Rose moved here with her Aunt when she was 15. She never said what happened to her parents and no-one ever asked. She was always so full of life and so beautiful. Bloom's the spitting image of her except she has Michael's eyes. People seemed to gravitate towards Rose, especially Michael. Except unlike with her other admirers she noticed him back."

"They started dating about a month after she arrived in town and stayed together all through high school. They were that annoyingly perfect couple. Michael proposed on graduation night and of course Rose accepted. They waited a year to the date to get married. Just enough time for Michael to build this house for them to live in. His Dad gave him the land as a graduation present and we all helped him work on building the perfect home for them. The wedding was beautiful. I'd never seen two people more in love than Michael and Rose."

"He got a job at the factory and she started taking classes at the college two towns over. On the weekends we'd all hang out and she'd try to fix me up with some girl she'd met in one of her classes. We were best friends and I loved them both like family."

"Then one morning I came out to the cabin to go hunting in the woods. Michael was working and he told me Rose would be in class so I didn't need to warn her I'd be there. I headed to my favorite spot and wasn't there very long before I heard rustling in the trees to my right. I turned and aimed my gun ready to shoot, expecting to see the buck I'd been leaving food out to attract. But it wasn't the buck. It was a glorious white wolf. I'd never seen a wolf up close but I knew wolves could be dangerous so I cocked my gun ready to take it out before it could attack. The wolf must have heard the gun cock because she turned and stared me in the eyes. I didn't notice the color I was so concerned with keeping the gun aimed between us. If I'd been thinking I would've realized no normal wolf had eyes the shade of emeralds. Then the wolf shifted and there at the end of my barrel was Rose."

"I dropped the gun and just stared. I was in such shock that I didn't say anything as she guided me back out of the woods toward the house. I still didn't speak as she sat me at the kitchen table with a cup of coffee and went and got dressed. Finally when she sat down across from me with a cup of her own I asked how. She explained everything; well at least what I thought was everything at the time."

"We sat there for hours, me asking questions and her answering. Finally she told me Michael didn't know. I was shocked because I thought they shared everything and here she'd kept this huge secret. I told her she had to tell him, that he'd understand. He loved her no matter what. That's when she told me she was pregnant. Only a few weeks along and she hadn't even told him yet. She wanted to wait till after the baby was born to tell him about being a shifter. I didn't want to add any stress to a pregnant woman so I agreed to keep her secret as long as she told him after the baby was here. She agreed."

"Bloom was born 9 months later. She was the most beautiful baby and already had a head full of blonde hair. Michael and Rose were so happy they were glowing. I was at the restaurant getting some food together to bring to the new parents when I got a call from Michael. Rose was gone, had left the hospital, went to the house grabbed a few things and wrote him a half ass letter about not being ready to be what he needed. Michael was devastated. Bloom was released from the hospital the next day and I was there to help Michael bring her home. He was broken though he tried to hide it. I helped the best I could. I'd watch Bloom when he was at work and would stick around after he got home to try to cheer him up. Eventually he came back around but he was never the same man."

"About 4 months after she left, Rose showed back up when Michael was at work. She begged me to see Bloom but I wouldn't let her without an explanation. She confessed that she'd met her mate at the hospital the day after she had Bloom. She couldn't resist the pull the mate bond had and she left with him. She loved Michael but love couldn't even describe her bond with this man. She wanted to take Bloom, she was worried she'd start to shift when she got older and Michael wouldn't have a clue what to do. I couldn't let her take her though. I loved that baby girl too much and I knew it would kill Michael to lose her too."

"She argued with me but didn't try to fight me on it, but she made me promise that if she showed any of the signs of shifting that I'd track her down in Tennessee. And if Bloom ever got hurt that I wouldn't take her to a regular doctor I'd take her to Jim Harris, the local vet. Apparently he had come across her and her aunt's secret like I had and was the only other person in town she trusted to care for Bloom. The regular doctors would start asking too many questions if Bloom's shifter blood kicked in and she healed at a speedy rate. I agreed to her terms but made her promise not to show back unless I called on her. It would be way too hard on Michael if she kept showing up. She agreed and I've not seen or heard from her since. Bloom's never shown a sign of shifting. Though I do believe some of Rose's shifter genes kicked in because she's never been sick a day in her life, not even a runny nose."

Finished telling me his story he picks the album back up and places it back in the box. He closes the shed up and then turns to me, "Pike I can tell you're her mate. I already see your presence healing her heart. The loss of her father devastated her but since you've arrived I've seen her smile again. A real genuine smile and I haven't seen that in a year. Just make sure you treat her right and don't keep her away from me too long. She's like my own child."

I can't reply without shifting so I give him a nod and hope he takes that as my agreement to care for her. This man has kept Rose's secret for over 19 years and as he's telling it to me. I swear I see his shoulders relax as the burden's lifted and my shoulders sag when he places it on mine. He's giving me the responsibility of telling Bloom about her Mom being a shifter. I guess I'll just figure a way of throwing that in there when I shift and inform her I'm her mate. How hard could it be?

Hey, I'm a wolf shifter and you're my mate. Oh and that mom that abandoned you when you were born, she's a wolf shifter too. And she's part of my pack. So you have shifter blood and you should be shifting into a wolf but for some reason you're not. Ready to run away from your home and take your place as my mate?

Damn Billy! He should've told her about Rose long before now. He stands there and watches my inner turmoil at my new task and begins to chuckle, "Not an easy task you have pup."

I huff and that brings another chuckle rolling out of him. It's nice to see that now that the burden's off of him he can go back to being the light hearted uncle figure, but he better realize he'll be helping me explain.

Chapter 14 – Bloom

~ King of Jerks ~

I wake up on Thursday with Pike's cold nose on my neck. He seems to be watching me constantly. I woke up the night before to get a drink of water and there Pike was watching and waiting on me before my feet were even out of bed. It's like he thinks if he's not right beside me something will happen. He's become protective that way, which's surprisingly fine by me. I feel at ease when he's with me. Some might say I'm craving company of any kind since Dad's death, but I think I've had plenty of people around just none as comforting as Pike.

I give him a quick scratch behind the ears then roll out of bed. I rush through my morning routine with him by my side, so I can start getting the fishing supplies together. Today we're going to the party at the lake with Bonnie.

After getting the poles and tackle box organized and packed into the truck, I start making a lunch for us. I toss slices of turkey to Pike as I put together the sandwiches and even cut up an apple to feed him. He won't touch the dog food I bought him at the vet's office, but he's all too happy to eat whatever I'm eating.

We're just finishing up a second apple when my cell phone starts to play the ringtone I have programmed for Bonnie. I dig it out of my pocket and hit the talk button, "Hi Bon! What time will you be here?"

"I'll be there soon. I thought we'd hang out till it's time to go."

"I'd love to Bon. We're just having lunch so I'll make you a sandwich too."

"Make me two I'm starved. See you in a few."

"Okay, two it is. See ya and be careful," I reply then end the call. I make Bonnie's two sandwiches and cut her up an apple to go with them. By the time I have put everything away and wiped down the counters she's pulling into the driveway and bouncing up the steps.

I hold the screen door open for her, "Your sandwiches are on the table. What do you want to drink?"

Slipping into the seat where I set her plate, "Got any sweet tea?"

"Do you even need to ask? Of course I do."

"I figured as much. I'll take a glass of that please," She mumbles around a mouth full of apple.

I pour us both a glass and sit down in the seat across from her. "So who'll be at this party tonight?"

She swallows her apple and then says, "Well most of the people from our graduating class and maybe a couple others. Why, is there someone in particular you're hoping to see?"

"Oh no, nothing like what you're thinking."

"And what am I thinking Bloom Michael?"

"That I want to see one of those skeezy guys we graduated with because I have some long harbored crush that I've been keeping from you. Well you can get that out of that cute little head of yours Bonnie Anne Harris. I'd rather eat my own toenails then date one of those guys."

"Your own toenails, really Bloom? They aren't that bad. Trace is easy on the eyes and he seems to have taken a shine to you."

Trace Clark, hearing his name makes my skin crawl. He comes across as one of the sweet country boys but he definitely isn't. He's hotheaded and arrogant. And he did not enjoy being turned down by me. We dated a few times but nothing came from it. It didn't take me long to learn that Trace likes to collect women like Jay Leno collects cars. And I wasn't interested in being his shiny new car. Last time I saw him was about 3 weeks before Dad died. I'd agreed to go to his friend's party with him, but we never made it that far. He pulled over on one of the side roads and attempted to stick his tongue down my throat and his hand up my shirt. Luckily I had my handy little mace keychain and sprayed him right in the eyes before hopping out of his pick-up and walking home. I haven't seen him since and I never thought to tell anyone what had happened. I was a little too embarrassed that I fell for his lies in the first place.

"Trace can find someone else to take a shine to because I'm not interested. Trust me Bon he's the king of the jerks, you need to stay clear of him."

"Okay, okay! It's not me that he's interested in anyways, it's you. But I definitely wouldn't choose my toenails over him."

"Subject change!" I cry ready for a new topic.

"No fair! There's something you're not telling me Bloom Michael Daniels and I want to know what it is," she says shaking her finger at me.

"Okay fine I'll tell you but seriously you can't tell anyone, especially not Billy or your Dad. They would freak out."

"Promise! Now spill." I relay the story of Trace trying to jump me in his truck and then wait for her response.

"That jerk off! Why didn't you tell me before?" She asks and I can see the hurt and anger brewing behind her eyes. Of course she's upset with me for keeping such a huge secret but I'm pretty sure the anger towards Trace was winning out. She may be sweet and bubbly most of the time but get on her bad side and she'll rip you apart and not think twice about doing so.

"I would've Bon, but I was embarrassed that I fell for his lines."

"You couldn't have known Blu. I can see why you don't want Dad and Billy to know though. They'd tear him limb from limb then leave his remains for the wild animals to dine on."

"They're just a little protective," I say smiling at the thought of my two adopted father figures.

"That's an understatement," Bonnie laughs then becoming serious says, "We don't have to go to the lake tonight. Trace will probably be there."

"No we're going Bon. I'm not letting him scare us away. You've been excited about it for days now. He wouldn't dare try something with so many witnesses. Plus it's been a year, he's probably set his sights on someone else."

"Are you sure? We could hang around here if it would be too uncomfortable," she politely offers though I can see she'd rather be at the lake. Not that I blame her, I've started looking forward to it as well.

"No I want us to go. And if he does try something you can just take him down with your mad ninja skills."

"Yes, I know I'm a ninja master. All five foot nothing of me could easily take down his over six foot frame. Easy peasy!" She tries to say in a menacing voice but can't do so without laughing hysterically.

"For a shorty you can be pretty scary at times Bon," I state trying to keep a straight face.

"Hey now don't be doubting us shorties, we play dirty and take out the knees first."

"I'd never doubt those scary knee breaking skills of yours."

Throwing a slice of her apple at my head, "Oh hush! This subject is closed. I think it's time you go pick out what you want to wear tonight so we can see if I approve."

"Are you insinuating that I can't dress myself?"

Looking me up and down, "Well Blu, if we're judging on who wears country chic the best you'd win hands down, but I do believe it's time we give the tank tops and jeans a break. Do you even own a skirt?"

"Does a jean skirt count?"

Massaging her temples to ease the imaginary headache I'm apparently causing, "No, Blu, it does not count. Now go into that room of yours and dig up something that isn't made of denim."

"You do realize we're going to the lake not a fashion show, right?" I ask as I get up to comply with her order.

"There's no time like the present to start dressing more like a girl than like a farm hand."

Chapter 15 – Pike

~ Considering her weak is a little bit of an understatement ~

Bloom's just left the room and I'm attempting to follow when her friend stops me in my tracks.

"Not so fast Alpha!" I turn to face her and watch as her normally soft expression hardens and her eyes narrow on me. "Daddy warned me the big bad wolf was in town searching for his little red riding hood."

I should've known Mr. Harris would warn Bonnie, but my mind's been too preoccupied to even consider the possibility. I turn to face her knowing I might as well get this one sided talk over with now. She leans forward so her face is close enough for me to hear her whisper. When I finally do shift I'll have to teach this girl about self preservation around wolf shifters. You'd think these people would realize it's not safe to challenge an Alpha; I can rip this weak girl's heart out before she could blink twice. Not that I will, of course, but geez a little respect would be nice.

"Yes, I know what you want with my best friend and exactly what you are. I also know how dangerous you are, but if you hurt my friend or let her be hurt in anyway, you will be held accountable by me and my .22. I can very easily make some silver bullets to shoot your hairy behind with, so watch your step, Wolf!"

Okay, maybe considering her weak is a little bit of an understatement. But it makes my heart happy to know my mate has friends like Bonnie. I lock eyes with her hoping my message will come across and give my silent promise to keep our Bloom safe with a nod of my head. The harshness in her face eases back to its normal soft features and she nods back.

"How about this dress, Bon? No denim in sight," Bloom asks walking back into the kitchen wearing a soft green sun dress that falls just above her knees. It brings out the green in her hazel eyes and if I were in my human form I'd probably drop to my knees begging to touch those long silky smooth legs that I can't take my eyes off of.

Bonnie gets up and circles her taking in the dress from all angles then says, "Well it's pretty simple but with the right accessories, it could work. Come on lets go find a belt." She grabs her hand and proceeds to drag her back in the direction of Bloom's room. Figuring they'd like some privacy I push open the screen door and make my way to the woods. I have to come up with a plan on how to reveal my true self to my mate and soon, and I think best when I'm running in my four legged form.

Chapter 16 – Bloom

~ It practically screams wear me to a lake party ~

Sitting on my bed with my legs crossed at the ankles I ask, "Is a belt really necessary?"

Bonnie's tearing through my closet throwing its contents all over my floor and as much as I love the girl I'm about to pull her away. I just cleaned my room the day before and now it looks like it hasn't been touched in a month.

"We've already went over this, a belt could make that dress perfect! I know you have just the right one, I bought it for you two Christmas' ago. I just have to find the darn thing. You didn't get rid of it did you?" She questions as she continues the attack on my closet.

"Of course I didn't." At least I don't think I did.

"Oh I think I found it. It's stuck. Ugh!" I watch as she yanks hard on the end of the belt she's holding and then falling backwards onto her butt and screams, "I got it!"

"Well that's good. Are you going to help me clean up this mess you made?"

Standing up she takes a survey of the mess she's made of my once clean room. "I'll come over tomorrow and help you clean it up but right now you need to stand up so we can try this on with your dress."

"Bonnie, I'm going to look silly wearing a dress to the lake," I try to protest.

"It's just a cotton sun dress, it practically screams wear me to a lake party. Now stand up."

Sliding off the bed I groan, "Why are we friends again?"

"If you didn't have me you'd probably be walking around in boring old jeans and t-shirts all the time. I add a bit of style to your life and though you complain about it, I know deep down you love that about our friendship. Just like I love that you add a little bit of country to mine. So hush up and put this belt on." She throws the belt at me with a smile on her face.

Putting the belt on I admit, "Okay, that's true. I do love you. So how does it look?"

Scrunching up her brow and rubbing her chin she looks me over then says, "Add in those brown cowboy boots you own and it'll be perfect!"

"So what are you wearing?"

"What I have on."

Taking in her jean skirt, peach colored tank top, and sandals I yell in protest, "Not fair! You're wearing a jean skirt."

"So? I look cute don't I?" She asks checking herself out in the mirror on my closet door.

"You look good, but you said no jean material."

"I said YOU couldn't wear jeans, not me. I don't need to change up my outfit routine; you on the other hand needed an outfit overhaul."

Throwing myself back on to the bed I complain, "So not fair."

Sitting down next to me and fiddling with the edge of my comforter, "You'll get over it. So how are things going with Pike?"

"Good, I feel calmer since he's been here. I know this might sound weird but I talk to him like he's a human and Bon I'd swear he understands me."

"I don't think it sounds weird Blu. So are you thinking about keeping him around?"

"I don't think I could get rid of him if I wanted to. He seems to have attached himself to my side."

"That's an understatement. Does he even give you alone time to bathe?" She asks giggling.

"Hey, he's not always with me. He's not here now!"

"The only reason he's not is because we drove him away with our girly talk of clothes."

"Bon, you do realize we're talking about Pike like he's some guy I'm dating."

"Yeah, I've noticed," she replies.

"Honestly, I think if it came down to me having to choose between him and a real boyfriend, I'd choose Pike," I confess.

"That makes sense."

Confused I turn to her and ask, "How so? I'm starting to think I'm losing touch with reality. You might have to commit me."

She quietly watches out my bedroom window for a few minutes and then finally speaks, "Bloom, there's something I think I need to tell you about Pike."

"What is it?"

"He ..." She's cut off by the sound of Pike howling outside. I run to the back door worrying he's hurt but find him okay, pawing at the back door.

Coming up behind me Bonnie asks, "Is everything okay?"

"Yeah, he must have got out the screen door and wanted back in. He's fine. So what was it you wanted to tell me about him?" I ask running my hands through the fur on the back of Pike's neck.

She watches Pike intently as she replies, "Oh um … just that you should probably give him a bath. He's starting to smell ripe."

"Really? I think he smells wonderful. Like the trees after a storm, all fresh and woodsy," I say leaning down into his neck to take in his scent.

"Wow! Did you just smell him like you would a bouquet of flowers? You seriously have been cooped up with that dog too long. I think it's time we head to the lake you need some more human to human interaction. People should be getting there by now anyways," she says rolling her eyes at me.

"You seriously can't smell that wonderfully woodsy scent on him?"

"No Bloom, and as tempting as it is to sit here all night watching you sniff Pike, I'd really rather go to the lake so I can check out some of those hot country boys we went to school with. So get your cute little behind off the floor so we can leave."

"Just let me grab my boots," I say standing up then ask. "Are you riding with us or following?"

"Following, that way if one of us wants to leave early the other won't have to leave too."

"Sounds like a plan."

An hour later I'm pulling into my favorite fishing spot. The lake's filling up with all of my old high school friends and I see a few are gathering wood to make a bonfire when it gets dark. There are a handful of guys already set up on the bank fishing and a group of girls not far from them standing around talking. Bonnie already parked and is making her way to the group of girls anxious to join in the gossip. Climbing out of my truck I hold the door open for Pike then begin unloading my fishing gear.

I cast out my last line then decide I might as well join the girls. Other than Bonnie I don't know the girls very well, we hung around the same circles in school but I'm not close to any of them. A couple give me a nod acknowledging me and one who's obviously feeling the effects of the beer in her hand throws her arms around my neck pulling me into an awkward hug. Pulling her off me Bonnie innocently directs her attention at someone else, "Jenna, I think I just saw Paul pull-in. Didn't you tell me you were looking for him?"

Looking around she slurs, "Yeah, where is he?" She locks eyes on her target in the parking lot, and then straightens up and trying to do her sexiest walk heads his way.

Glancing over at Bonnie I catch her attention and mouth, "Thank you!"

She mouths back, "Any time," then goes back to her conversation with the girl beside her.

"Poor Paul, he has no clue Hurricane Jenna's about to hit him," Maddy the girl beside me giggles.

"I feel bad for him, but I really didn't want her spilling that beer down my back," I say smiling at Maddy.

"So what's your dog's name?"

Looking at Pike standing at attention beside me I reply, "Oh this is Pike."

"Cool name, so what kind of dog is he?"

"I'm not sure. I found him hurt in the woods beside my house a few days ago and he's just been with me since. Mr. Harris thinks he might be a wolf hybrid."

"Wow that's nice of you to take him in. I'd have been frightened to go near him if I'd seen him in the woods. He's just so large!"

"I didn't even think of him being dangerous. I heard his howls and just felt the need to help." Thinking about it I guess it is strange that I didn't question running into the woods. Who honestly does something like that? Most people would've heard the howl and ran inside, but I felt the need to go to him and help.

Breaking into my inner rambling Maddy says, "Well you're definitely braver than me."

"Maybe," I reply clearly distracted. Can it be that simple? Did I not question it because I'm braver? It seems like something more yet I can't quite put my finger on it. I look down at Pike and his eyes are on mine. Those ocean blue eyes that are so breath-taking and seem to have way more knowledge behind them than a dog should have.

"Blu, don't look now but Trace just arrived," Bonnie whispers in my ear at the same time Pike breaks eye contact and turns his attention towards the parking lot.

"He isn't coming this way is he?" I ask turning to look at her instead of searching out Trace. I need to make sure he's a safe distance from me. When she doesn't answer right away I ask again, "He isn't coming over here is he, Bonnie?"

Hearing me use her full first name instead of the abbreviation I've used ever since we were kids or maybe it's the shaky way my voice is coming out, she finally brings her attention back to me. "No, he's not coming over … yet. But he hasn't taken his eyes off you since he noticed your truck in the parking lot."

"Crap! I really hope he isn't moronic enough to make a scene with everyone here."

"He has that oh so perfect reputation to uphold so I doubt he will."

"That's true, he likes everyone to think he's the good guy."

I keep my distance from Trace and keep Pike and Bonnie by my side until it starts getting darker. Most of the people are gravitating towards the now roaring bonfire or sneaking off into the woods for some alone time. Bon just happens to be in that last group. She found herself the attention of her high school crush and is now having a nice "talk" behind some trees. So I'm sitting here on the bank with Pike trying to keep my distance from the rowdy group by the fire, which just so happens to include Trace. Every time tonight I've taken the chance to make sure he's a safe distance away I find his eyes watching me and a wicked grin spread across his face. How I ever fell for that good guy act I don't know. Seeing him now there's no question that he's bad, and not in that bad boy you want to save way either. More like the bad guy you'll find on the evening news after bodies are found in his back yard kind of way.

I make sure he isn't paying attention as I sneak off into the dark to do some fishing. The moon isn't out so the lake's covered in darkness so I know he can't see me from his position by the fire. Taking comfort in that knowledge I settle down in the grass with Pike by my side.

Running my fingers through Pike's coat I feel him tense under my hand. Is he actually growling at me? No, he wouldn't. Looking around I feel like growling myself when I see who Pike has his gaze locked on.

Walking right towards us with that cocky grin on his face is Trace.

I snap back to reality when I feel Pike stand and growl with his ears pinned back. Dang, dogs really can sense the bad guys. Keeping my hand grazing over his fur and trying to show no emotion I look up and ask Trace, "What do you want?"

"We have some unfinished business Bloom, so I thought I'd come keep you company and we can finish what we started." There's a wicked gleam in his eyes that sends a shiver down my spine.

Not wanting to look weak I stand and look him dead in the eye and ask, "How can you be this thick headed? What from our last encounter would make you think I wanted to spend time with you ever again? Let alone finish what *you* unsuccessfully tried to start." Moving to stand in between Trace and myself, Pike dips low ready to pounce with a growl rumbling low in his throat.

"Now come on Blu you know I was just playing. Just call off your mutt and we can talk this out." He's actually brave enough to take a step forward. But Pike's right there to cut him off from coming any closer snapping his jaws at him. Gosh, I'd miss him if someone comes to claim him.

Anger seeping into my voice. "One, only my family and friends calls me Blu and you are neither. Two, Pike is not a mutt. Three, stay the hell away from me, Trace. I'm not interested!" To send the point home Pike lets out a ferocious growl. Trace puts his hands up in defeat and starts backing away. He's pissed and it shows clearly on his face that he isn't giving up, but I'm not going to worry about that right now. Pike's won me this battle.

As soon as Trace's a safe distance away and clearly not coming back Pike relaxes and comes back over and rubs up against my side. I slide back down onto the bank and rest my head against his side. I can't help but think that if I can find a guy half as loyal and caring as this dog I'd marry him in a heartbeat. I chuckle at myself. Did I really just wish I could find a guy that acted like a dog? That has to be a first; usually we want them to stop acting like dogs.

Chapter 17 – Pike

~ How? ~

I can see in her mind and feel her emotions. I was listening when she told Bonnie what happened but seeing what that jerk tried to do to her, through our mate bond, has made my wolf crave his blood. Thankfully I also saw what she did to him; it was smart of her carrying that spray. She wasn't frightened though most women in that situation would've been, she was mad and not even at him. She was mad at herself for being such a fool. She's way too hard on herself. I want to hurt this guy for making her question herself. If she hadn't been right there watching me I would have ripped him apart, but the last thing I want to do is scare her. I'm already worried how she's going to react when I reveal my true self to her.

I've lain beside her every night for a week. I've watched her sleep and breathed in that sweet scent of hers; strawberries and cedar. Even now surrounded by the smells of this lake and the fish living in it, I can smell her strawberry and cedar scent strongest. I could smell her from miles away. I did, that's how I found her and how I got caught in that damn trap. I was consumed with finding where that heavenly scent originated and wasn't paying attention. I haven't been able to be far from her side since the moment I found her. My heart aches for her closeness and my wolf's protective of her. My pack would laugh at me now if they saw me playing "pet," but I have to get to know her and find away to reveal mine and now Billy's secrets without scaring her away.

I can hear her thoughts seeping into my mind, they are washed in exhaustion. She hates arguments; they seem to drain her as much as I seem to relax her. She's glad I'm here to protect her and she's hoping she doesn't see this guy again, but she knows it's not over. I wish I could shift and pull her into my arms to comfort her, but that would just cause her more stress.

Instead I just rub up against her side, knowing that's the best I can do at this time.

She's leaning against me now and is knotting her hands in my fur. I can't wait to have her hands in my hair that way, and mine in hers. I'm brought back out of my fantasy by more of her thoughts. Wait did she just say she'll marry me? No, she's just wishing she could find a man who was like me and said she'll marry him if she does. I have to chuckle at that though. She already has and doesn't even know it. Though I wish she'll quit calling me a dog. I can't really blame her for that; I've been the one playing the good "dog." I need to work up the courage I know I have and show her she already has me.

How do you break it to the woman you love that the "dog" she has come to care for isn't a dog at all, but a man who can change into a wolf? I could shift right in front of her so she won't be able to accuse me of being insane, but she'll probably think she's lost it instead.

Chapter 18 – Bloom

~ She'll burn you faster than the Florida sun in July ~

By the time Bonnie comes back from her "talk" and finds me it's after midnight. I'm drained from the confrontation with Trace, but I don't want to worry her so I don't bring it up. She's clearly having a good time. Her lips are bruised pink from being freshly kissed and the smile hasn't left her face since she sat down beside me. Knowing she's ready to relay what's happened to me but not wanting to brag I go ahead and ask, "So on a scale of 1 to 10, how good of a kisser is he?"

Watching the dark water on the lake trying to hide that her smile has somehow grown wider, "Hmm, I'd say he's a 6."

Shocked I ask, "A 6 has put that smile on your face?"

"A six is a decent kiss rating."

"A six is average. The smile you have should only come from a kiss that rates at least a 9 if not a perfect 10. So please explain what's causing this reaction."

"I'm smiling because I've realized that all those years I crushed on him I could've had him and now I don't want him. It's funny how things work out."

"Let me get this straight. You're smiling because he wants you and you don't want him?"

"I know it sounds mean, but it feels nice to be wanted even though I know now he's not what I want."

"Not mean Bon that's just the way it goes sometimes. You've had this perfect idea of what he would be like for four years and now you're just realizing he doesn't live up to the dream him. Plus he's been on the receiving end of being wanted for four years without stepping up so it's about time you got your turn to feel wanted back," I tell her putting my arm around her shoulders.

Laying her head against mine she says, "Thanks for not thinking I'm an awful person."

"Bon I could never think that. We both know it's my job to be the mean one." I lay my head a top hers.

"True. Do you remember what you did in junior high when I got my first period in gym class and Sarah Jenkins made fun of me? That was mean." She laughs at the memory.

"I waited till lunch then pretended to trip and dumped my tray all over her favorite white sweater. There was no way she could've got that spaghetti stain out. But she deserved it, we girls are supposed to have each other's backs when it comes to those issues and that witch broke girl code." Thinking back on the memory still makes me laugh too. If someone messed with Bonnie they had to deal with me and vice versa.

Bonnie may come across as pure sunshine but if you think that means she's weak you're wrong. If you mess with her family or me, she'll burn you faster than the Florida sun in July.

"Sorry I left you alone with Trace on the prowl. He didn't bother you, did he?" Crap! I really hate lying to Bonnie, but I can't bring myself to make her feel guilty for going off and enjoying herself.

"Nope, no sign of him," I lie.

"Good. I wouldn't want to have to use my mad ninja skills and take out his knees." She laughs striking her seriously funny version of a ninja pose.

"Oh my gosh! Those are some killer moves. Remind me to never get on your bad side."

"I'll try. Well I'm going to go back and join the bonfire, maybe roast a marshmallow or two. You want to join me?"

"As much as I love the gooey wonderfulness that is a toasted marshmallow, I think I'll take a rain check. I'm going to head home so I can pass out." Standing up I take her hand and pull her to her feet.

"If you insist, but make sure you text me when you get home." She pulls me into a tight hug.

Hugging her back I say, "I can handle that as long as you do the same. I don't care if it's four in the morning you better text me."

"I will. See you tomorrow!"

"See ya Bon!" I watch her to make sure she makes it back to the group without any trouble then pack up my gear. Reaching the truck and holding open the door I call, "Come on Pike. Let's head home."

We're only a few miles away from the lake when I notice a vehicle behind us is driving way to close. I slow down trying to give them a chance to pass, but they just slow up and stay right on my tail. I speed up and they speed up too. We play this back and forth for about 4 miles and we're nearing a curve when I notice the vehicle slip into the other lane to pass, but he doesn't pass. He pulls right up beside me and I realize it's Trace behind the wheel.

He rams the jeep into the side of my truck running me off the road and into the ditch. I'm luckily wearing my seat belt and we don't hit hard enough for the air bags to deploy but Pike's thrown into the front floor pretty hard and doesn't seem to be moving. Unfastening my seatbelt I try to reach for him to check on him, but as soon as I'm loose I hear the door open and I'm jerked from my seat.

Trace wraps his arm around my chest and presses something hard and cold against my temple. With pure hatred in his voice, "Now we'll finish what we started!" My brain's racing. How can I get out of this and make sure Pike's alright and is this jerk really holding a gun to my head? I guess I should be afraid but I feel eerily calm. My voice dripping with sarcasm, "You know if you wanted something from me you could've just asked. No need to dent my fender."

I hope my lack of fear shocks him enough to give me some kind of opening to get loose but Trace isn't completely stupid. He tightens his grip digging his rough fingers into my side. There'll be a bruise there but it might be the least of my injuries if I don't get away.

His lips are pressed to my ear when he says, "After tonight my little flower you'll never want another man again." He sucks my earlobe into his mouth as the hand holding the gun leaves my head and he drags it down my side. I know I have to get away or I'll never be able to get this night out of my head, if he even lets me live past it.

When his lips start trailing down my neck he loosens his grip around my chest enough to grab roughly onto my breast. I know now is probably the only chance I'll get so I attempt to slam my heel into his foot. In my mind it gives me the chance to get loose so I can run, in reality it doesn't do anything but anger the prick because he's wearing steel-toed work boots. He throws me hard onto the ground and levels the gun at me with one hand as he's using the other to undo his jeans. My stomach's rolling. I know it won't be long before its contents come back up. I turn my head away from the monster in front of me not wanting him to see how much he's upsetting me. He may be able to strip me of what I have guarded for the last 20 years but there's no way I'm letting him think this will break me. The vomit starts to come up and I swallow it back down. I'm fighting back the second wave of sickness when I catch movement in the truck. I tempt a glance back at Trace to see if he noticed. Nope, he's too busy working his pants down with one hand. Turning back to the truck the movement's gone. Maybe I imagined it.

I'm brought out of my thoughts when I feel the weight of Trace on top of me, effectively pinning me to the ground. There's no way I'll be able to get him off of me from this position. My hands are still free but I can't see anything within my reach that could hurt him enough to get away. He begins pulling my dress up my body stopping every few inches to rub his sweaty hands along my legs then my stomach. Realizing his hands are both gun free I desperately search the ground for the gun. He has it tucked up against his side near his pants. If I stretch I may be able to reach it before he realizes what's going on. I stretch my hand over the hard ground trying to move as little as possible so he won't notice. My fingers just feel the cold metal of the barrel when it's ripped away from my grasp.

"You little whore! You thought you could use my own gun on me." Then he slams the butt of the gun down hard against my temple.

The pain's so intense and the black's already starting to cloud my eyes or maybe I'm closing them, I'm not sure which one's happening. I want to let the darkness take me away to a safe place ….

Growling, why is there growling in my darkness? I fight my eyelids to get them to open back up and focus. I notice that Trace's weight is no longer on top of me so I attempt to sit up. The pain radiating through my head is so intense I about fall back to the ground. I grip my knees to keep my upper half from falling backwards. Once I feel fairly certain I won't pass back out I raise my head from my knees to survey the scene before me.

Pike! He has Trace backed up to the edge of the road. There's no doubt in me now that he's a wolf, he's a predator and Trace is his prey. He stalks the monster that attacked me. He's not looking for his opening, he already has that. What's he doing?

Chapter 19 – Pike

~ You have a lot more to worry about than my creative story telling ~

My wolf is savoring the taste of his fear. Even if I can't taste it in the air I'd still be able to see it in the way his hand is shaking around the gun handle. He doesn't have it pointed at me and I want to keep it that way. It's time I take him out so I can get to my mate. I hear her come to but I don't want to draw his attention to that, he might try to take aim at her.

I take a few steps towards him and I'm getting ready to pounce when the lights on the road catch both of our attention. Great! Just what I need, some silly human getting in the way of me helping my mate.

The car slams on its brakes and I hear the door fly open. The driver comes running our way and I think she might throw herself at me, but thankfully she runs to my mate. Falling on to her knees, Bonnie pulls

Bloom into her arms. I let out a sigh of relief. My mate's being cared for so I don't have to worry about leaving her side to take care of the trash in front of me.

I turn back towards my prey but he's no longer in front of me. He's made it to the still running car Bonnie arrived in. The coward's using the drivers' side door as a shield and he has the gun pointed at me. There's a smug look on his face when he pulls the trigger. I try to high tail it out of the bullets path but it catches my shoulder and I stagger to the ground. I pull myself back to my feet; I'm not going to let this bastard think I'm weak, and take off after the car. He's briefly stunned by my being able to take a bullet and still come for him but before I can reach him he jumps into the car and slams the door shut. I'm desperately trying to rip the door off the hinges to get to him when he throws the car into drive and takes off.

I want to chase after him, I can easily catch up with the car, but I need to get back to Bloom. She passed out again when the gun went off and taking care of her comes before taking my revenge on her attacker. I make a promise to myself that I will hunt him down and make him pay. I keep my eyes on the retreating tail lights as I back myself up in the direction where I know my mate lays unconscious.

"Alpha, get your tail over here!" Bonnie impatiently calls for me. Feeling the threat's out of the way for now, I turn and cross the remaining distance. The soft green dress Bloom put on earlier in the day is now a dirt covered mess that has rips stretching from the bottom hem up to her hip. Her beautiful legs are covered in scrapes and bruises that seem to already be healing. Her hair is falling out of the braid she styled it into and has grass and twigs matted in it. And there on her temple I can see the bruising and swelling from where the gun connected. She's healing from the injury, her shifter blood is making sure of that, but she may never emotionally recover from what almost happened to her tonight.

"Pike, you need to shift. She needs to been seen by my Dad and I can't carry her," Bonnie pleads.

I give Bonnie a quick nod so she knows I hear what she's saying then I will the change to take me over. It starts at my back paws cracking and rearranging my bones then slowly works its way up my body. I'm already standing on two legs when I feel my muzzle shorten and my face start to take shape. Finally I feel my ears shorten and my sharp wolf senses dull and I know the change has finished.

Ignoring the fact that I'm naked I bend down and take my mate from Bonnie's arms. She's breathing steady but she's still unconscious. The knot on the side of her head is already going down but I still want Mr. Harris to exam her. I have to suppress my growl when I think of that human touching her. They consider my kind monsters and look what one of theirs did to an innocent woman. I take a deep breath to calm my wolf then turn to Bonnie, "His vehicle's up by the road, please go see if the keys are in it. She's already healing but she still needs to be seen by your Dad."

Bonnie takes off towards the road and I cradle Bloom to my chest as I follow slowly not wanting to jar her and cause her anymore pain. If I have to lay down my life to guarantee it, she will never be in pain again. It might be an unattainable goal, but it's one I'm committed to achieving.

Standing by the back passenger door Bonnie holds out a gym bag to me, "I found these in the back. You might want to put them on, you know in case we get pulled over. I might be able to explain why we're in Trace's SUV, but I doubt I'll be able to explain a naked stranger holding my unconscious best friend."

I gently lay Bloom across the back seat then I take the bag from Bonnie. Taking cover at the rear of the vehicle I quickly dress then climb into the back seat with my mate placing her head in my lap. Bonnie has already taken the driver's seat and once I close my door she puts the big SUV into gear and heads us towards what I assume is her Dad's house.

Leaning my head back against the seat I close my eyes and let out the breath I hadn't even realized I was holding in. I could've lost her tonight without her ever knowing what she means to me. As soon as she's awake I'm spilling everything. No more hiding myself from the one person who can love me no matter what I am. I take one more deep breath and let it out, then look down at the woman who holds my future. Her hazel eyes, now more green than brown, are staring up at me. Not able to stop myself I brush my hand down her cheek and whisper, "Bloom, you're safe now. I'm here."

She's scanning my face, I can hear her thinking I look familiar to her; the mate connection causes that reaction. Her gaze falls to my lips and she wets her own, then she draws her eyes to mine and we both get lost looking at each other. Finally she hesitantly asks, "Who are you? Your eyes ... th-they look so familiar."

My wolf's screaming for me to answer, to spill everything and I want to but I don't want to send her into shock. She's already been through too much tonight. I need to wait till she's had time to heal and rest before I throw my news on her. Before I can come up with a response Bonnie takes over the conversation, "Blu, I'm taking you to my Dad and Billy. Do you remember being attacked?"

She tries to sit up but I hold her in my lap not yet ready to release her so she gives up and turns her head to Bonnie's gaze in the rear view mirror and with panic in her voice demands, "You didn't tell them what happened did you? Bonnie you can't tell them they'll freak out."

"Bloom they need to know."

"No they don't! Bonnie you got to promise you won't tell them what really happened. Please, for me?" She begs.

"Fine, I promise but just so you know I think they should be told."

"Thanks Bon," she sighs then turns snuggling closer into my chest and passes back out.

Wrapping my arms tighter around her I ask Bonnie, "What are we going to say happened, if we're not telling the truth?"

"We'll tell them she had a wreck, it's not really a lie we'll just be omitting what really caused the wreck and what happened after the wreck, but if she doesn't want them to know the truth I'll stand by her."

"That's an awful lot of omitting for it not being a lie."

Eyeing me from the rear view mirror Bonnie snaps, "You wanna know what wolf boy, you have a lot more to worry about than my creative story telling. You're gonna have to confess everything to her soon or she'll figure it out on her own. Her hair may be blonde but she's no ditz."

Looking down at Bloom's face I run my fingers along her hair line admiring the softness on my finger tips, "Bonnie, I almost lost her tonight and I want nothing more than to confess everything to her. I'd even get down on my knees and grovel for forgiveness for not telling her sooner. I just want her to be okay with it all." I catch the confused look she's giving me and realize she misunderstands what I'm saying so I clarify, "Not with what happened to her tonight. The physical signs are already fading; by tomorrow you won't even know he touched her. The emotional scars are going to take longer but with all of us who love her there to help her, she'll be able to heal those as well. I'm just worried that she'll reject our mating and who she truly is."

"She's already healing? I thought she wasn't a shifter!" Bonnie practically screams at my reflection in her mirror. "And is it even possible for her to reject the mating?"

"She hasn't changed like a normal shifter but she carries shifter blood in her and it's thankfully speeding up the healing process," I explain ignoring her last question.

"Well that's good I guess."

"Yeah it is."

"Don't think I didn't catch you ignoring the last question. So spill wolf! Can a person reject their mate?"

"It's not unheard of but it's very rare. Bonnie you have to realize that mates complement each other and if you reject your mate you're resigning yourself to a life of never feeling complete. You'd be rejecting the one person who would always love you the exact way you are, the person who was put on this earth for you and you alone. So to answer your question, yes a person could reject their mate but most don't because there's not a downside to being mated."

"Not unless you count that your "mate" turns furry at will."

"Well, yes, there is that little stipulation." I wait for her to ask more questions or give me another smart aleck reply but after a few minutes she seems finished and is focused on driving.

Then she asks, "Pike, what happens if one of the non-furry mates is allergic to dogs?"

"We're not dogs," I growl.

Chapter 20 – Bloom

~ One of a kind ~

Ocean blue ... the clearest water with its warm sun and its rainstorm scent.

Rainstorm?

That can't be right there's not a cloud in the sky, but still my ocean smells like home after a good summer storm has moved through, all fresh and woodsy. My ocean smells like Pike. Heck my ocean's even the same color as my furry best friends' eyes. I wonder why he isn't here with me, he wouldn't leave me alone. I call for him, "Pike! Where are you?"

I expect him to come to me but instead I get a reply, "Bloom, I'm right here."

Spinning around in the water looking for the person who's answering and finding no-one, I scream for Pike again.

Once again that voice replies, "Bloom, I'm right here. Open your eyes and you'll see I'm right here with you."

I do as the voice demands and find my ocean reflecting back at me from the strangers' eyes and just like in my dream I feel safe. I force my eyes away from his so I can take in the rest of him. The top of his head is covered in jet black hair that's shaggy and falling into his eyes. His nose is narrow and a little crooked at the bridge, it's probably been broken before. I have to grip the sheets under my hand to stop myself from reaching out and running my fingers over the crooked section. Forcing my eyes on I find his lips, the bottom is a tad fuller, the kind that begs to be kissed and nibbled on. As the thought crosses my mind his cheeks take on a soft blush. Did I say that out loud? No ... no, I didn't. But why is he looking at me like he knows exactly what I'm thinking.

Pushing that silly thought from my mind I continue perusing. He has a strong jaw with a five o'clock shadow. His shoulders are broad and connected to muscular arms. Gosh those arms. I want nothing more than for those arms to be wrapped around my body holding me to his well toned chest. Then my eyes travel further down his arms and I find his hands gripping my free hand. The one that isn't attached to the sheet; keeping me from making a fool of myself by caressing every clothes free section of skin of a complete stranger. Yet, he doesn't feel like a stranger. Why do I feel like I know him? Why do I feel like I can trust him with my life? And why the hell does he smell so darn good? Just like a summer storm ….

"Pike?!" I whisper.

Those unbelievably tempting lips spread into a wide smile revealing pearly white teeth and a dimple in each cheek. Then he speaks in a gravelly voice that melts me from the inside out, "Yes darlin', I'm Pike. And *we* have a lot to explain to you."

"We?" I ask looking around the room and finding that Pike and I aren't alone, though if he hadn't mentioned them I would've thoroughly enjoyed eating him up with my eyes for several more hours. But to my dismay Bonnie and her father are sitting at the foot of the bed, and Billy's standing across the room looking out the window. As if sensing my eyes on him, he turns and gives me a half-hearted smile and then says, "Blu, I have a story you need to hear."

I look back to the dimpled dark haired angel still holding my hand hoping that he can get me out of whatever "talk" Billy has for me, because the lord knows with the look he has on his face it won't be an enjoyable one and right now I want nothing more than to admire this man calling himself Pike. Yes, he has the same piercing eyes as my dog and apparently they share that unique name, but I'm not ready to hear the story yet, can't they see I just want to enjoy my ignorant bliss.

He squeezes my hand and practically reading my thoughts says, "I promise if you listen to what Billy has to say it will answer those questions that are floating around in your beautiful mind. And when he's done we can talk alone, if that's what you still want."

"Alright," I begrudgingly give in.

Thirty minutes later I'm left thunderstruck looking at the small group of people sitting around me. I'm half expecting someone with a hidden camera to jump out and say I've been punk'd, but after taking in each of their faces I realize no one's hiding to record my reaction. The alternative seems way more farfetched though. How can they expect me to believe such a story?

I look to Bonnie, she'd never lie to me, "Bonnie, please tell me the truth."

She comes over, sits beside me and says, "Blu, you know I wouldn't lie to you."

I nod in agreement.

"Well, I can't vouch for Billy's story about your mom," I give her a sharp look because she knows I don't refer to that woman that way and she amends, "I mean Rose. Because like you I've never met the woman, but as for Pike, I saw him shift from that black furry mutt."

Pike growls softly on my other side and once again my attention's drawn to those stormy eyes. But I know if I keep my attention on him I'll never hear the answers my friend is giving me. So I turn back to Bonnie and she continues like Pike's growling hasn't intimidated her, "Like I was saying. I watched him shift from that lovely beast who's been following you around all week to the man he is now. I wouldn't make that up, Blu. And I don't think Billy or my Dad would make up the stuff about Rose either."

"But Bon, if you're not making this up that means th-that Rose is a werewolf and so am I."

"We prefer shifter," Pike jumps in. "And though you haven't technically shifted, yet, you still carry that gene."

"Yet?" I ask a little frightened by the idea of myself sprouting fur and howling at the moon. *Don't be afraid.* I hear come through my thoughts and it sounds like me but somehow not me. Great now I'm hearing voices.

Pike grabs my hand again, in an attempt to comfort me. He already gave me the mate speech, after Billy told me about Rose, explaining what we are to each other, and that it gives him direct access to my thoughts and feelings. I wonder if he heard that voice inside me too. On one level I'm drawn to the idea, knowing this beautiful man I'm so attracted to is all mine, but then I find myself drifting to the other side that's screaming I didn't get the choice. My thoughts and feeling will never be private again. Will I ever get to the point where I'm comfortable with him knowing all my fears and insecurities? That other part of myself that seems to be fighting the wolf side (Could that be who the voice is, my wolf?) of myself, is feeling like I've been dropped naked in a room full of strangers for their viewing pleasure, and she doesn't like this one bit.

He waits for my inner monologue to cease then says, "Bloom, I know this might be a lot for you to take in after everything else you went through last night, but as your mate I promise to never keep anything from you."

"Well that's good to know. Why do you think I still may shift?" I ask still a frightened of his answer.

"Because the shifter gene's dominant. A mating between a shifter and a full human isn't uncommon, but if a child is born from the relationship it always comes out a shifter."

"There's always an exception to the rule, right? There has to be others like me, who heal faster than normal, but don't shift," I plead

"I can check with the pack elders when we go back to Tennessee, but as far as I know you're the only exception to that rule, darlin'."

"So not only am I getting thrust into a world that most people only believe is real in books, but apparently I'm a freak in this world as well. Great!" I reply sarcastically. I know I'm coming across extremely whinny, but seriously can you blame me. In a span of less than 12 hours I have been attacked by a psycho, saved by my pet who happens to be some kind of furry knight in shining armor, found out that the man I trusted like my own father kept a huge secret from me about my birth mother also going furry, and now they're telling me that I'm the odd one. So excuse me if I get a little whinny.

Reading my mind Pike smiles down at me, "Darlin', you're not odd; you're one of a kind."

"Blu, don't get down on yourself. Wolf boy's right, you are one of a kind and anyone that says different will have to deal with me," Bonnie adds, taking hold of my other hand. I smile at my friend. I've always thought I was the stronger of the two of us, since I've fought her fights more times than I can count, but I see she's just as fierce, she just doesn't need to show that side as often. Though I see she's decided it's the side she's showing to Pike, she apparently doesn't want the alpha wolf to see her as weak. I hope she doesn't make it a permanent change. I'd miss my sweet sunny Bonnie. While I'll probably always live in the darkness with my demons in one way or another, she'll always be the person who knows how to bring the light into my life. She's the sun to my moon, the sister I never had, simply put she's my best friend.

I let go of Pike's hand and pull Bonnie closer for a hug and whisper, "Thank you, Bon."

"Anytime, Blu." Then pulling back she says, "Now I think we need to give you and tall, dark and furry a chance to talk alone." Pike growls at the nickname and for the first time since the revelations I giggle. Mr. Harris gives me a quick hug and tells me to call him if I start to feel bad, which I promise to do. Then Billy kisses my cheek and apologizes once again for keeping the secrets from me. I take pity on the old guy and let him know I forgive him, which brings tears to his eyes. Bonnie ushers them both out and follows, but not before she promises to return to check on me the next day.

Once I hear the front door shut I become acutely aware I'm alone in my bedroom with Pike. He's still sitting at my bedside watching me intently. Feeling a little overwhelmed I hop out of bed thankful someone, probably Bonnie, had thought to remove my tattered sundress and put pajamas on me. Standing up against the wall by the door as far away from him as I can get I declare, "Umm ... I think I need to get cleaned up. You can go in the living room. I'll be in shortly and we can talk." Yeah, I know I'm real smooth. *It's ok, he's our mate. You don't have to win him over, we already have him.* Great, now I'm getting advice from the voice in my head.

Strutting over to me he stops and places one hand against the wall by my head and leans in close so our faces are less than an inch apart. That traitorous wolf half of me is screaming for him to kiss us, while the more sensible human half wants to kick him in the balls so he'll back up out of our personal space. *Come on; close the distance so we can see what his mouth tastes like.* My wolf pushes. I know he can hear my thoughts and they're probably what is causing the shit eating grin that he has plastered to his face. He leans in closer and I instinctively close my eyes and brace myself for his lips to touch mine, but it never comes. Instead when I open my eyes I find him smelling the crook of my neck. I surprise myself by being mad that he didn't kiss me.

"You smell so good, darlin', like fresh picked strawberries," he whispers when he steps back from me.

Exasperated I throw my arms up and growl, "Freaking shifters and your freaky smelling abilities! Go to the living room now so I can get cleaned up or you're sleeping on the porch tonight."

"No reason to get upset, darlin', I promise I'll kiss ya. I just want to wait till you can handle it." He chuckles at my outburst.

Glaring at him and pointing at the door, "Out!"

Holding up his hands in surrender he says, "Okay, but don't take long. We have a lot to discuss." Then he leaves my room.

Remembering something he said early I holler, "And I caught that Tennessee comment earlier and I am not going!" My wolf whimpers because she doesn't like that idea.

"Yes, you are!" He hollers back and the way it comes out I know it isn't up for discussion, which has my inner wolf smiling.

Chapter 21 – Pike

~ Our Dirty Little Secret ~

I pull out of her thoughts while she gets cleaned up. She needs the privacy so she can think through everything that's happened today and I need to gather my thoughts before we talk. I'd already explained our mate connection, but we have some decisions to make and I know she'll have questions. She may not see it now but I can feel the pull she has to me and no matter what she may say or think, I know she wants me with her just as much as I want to be with her. So she has to come home to Tennessee with me. I've already been gone from the pack too long and need to get back, and I'm not leaving here without her. My pack needs to meet their alpha's mate and we need to talk to the Elders about her not being able to shift. I'm hoping one of them has some insight. I'm happy with my mate either way, but I can feel how uneasy she was when she realized she should've shifted by now. I'm going to help my mate through all of these changes in her new life, it's the least I can do for her since she's going to let me love her.

"Pike, are you awake?" She asks softly causing me to open my eyes. I sat down on the couch to sort through my thoughts and I didn't even realize I'd closed them.

She crosses the room and sits at the other end of the couch facing me with her legs pulled up against her. Her hair's wet and braided down her back and her perfect face is clean of all make-up. The gash that had been on her head, from being hit with the gun, is already healed. She's wearing her favorite worn in jeans and a loose fitting white t-shirt. She's avoiding eye contact with me by picking at her perfectly manicured toe nails.

Turning to mirror her position I demand, "Darlin', look at me."

Her head snaps up and those brown-green eyes lock on mine and she sighs, "Okay."

"Bloom, tell me what you're thinking. Please."

"Can't you just pick it out of my brain?" She snaps back.

"Yes, I could." I sigh then say, "But I don't want to. I need *you* to tell me what you're thinking; I need you to trust me. I promise to give you as much privacy as possible, but sometimes I won't be able to. Until we complete are mate bond and learn to control our connection, your thoughts are going to be screaming at me. It's a way for me to protect you. Eventually you'll be able to block me when you need privacy. But until then I'll try to give you some mental privacy."

"Thank you," she says chewing her lip.

"Darlin', please tell me what's going through your mind?" I ask softly.

"Will I be able to read your mind?" she blurts out. The question makes me smile because it reassures me of how she feels even though I know she may not confess it just yet.

"I think so. You kind of already did."

"What? When?" She asks confused.

"Do you remember the night you found me in the woods?"

She nods.

"Well, when you were trying to figure out what to call me. I was screaming my name over and over in my head hoping that you'd be able to hear me. I really didn't want you to call me Fido or Rover.," I explain.

"Your name just seemed to come to me that night."

"Because you picked it up out of my thoughts and I think that now that you realize you can you'll be able to pick out my thoughts easier."

"Can we try?"

"Try what?" I ask confused.

"Me reading your thoughts," she says all giddy.

"Of course, darlin'. I'll think of something really hard and you try to focus on me. You should be able to pick it up," I suggest.

"Alright, let's try this Tennessee." She smiles at me before closing her eyes to focus.

I start with a simple word.

Mate.

I repeat it over and over in my head. When her eyes flew open and she has a smile stretching across her face I know she's heard it.

"Mate?" She asks confidently.

Smiling back I nod a confirmation then say, "Let's try something harder. How about I replay a memory and you see if you can pick it up and tell me about it."

"Okay," she says closing her eyes again.

This time I focus on the day I picked up her scent. I play the memory out until I had arrived at her house and then I repeat the memory over and over. Filling it with all of the emotions I'd been feeling that day. On the fourth rotation of the memory in my head she speaks without opening her eyes.

"You were running so fast and you had such a need," she whispers.

"I knew I'd found you, darlin'," I state.

"How can you be so sure?" she asks opening her eyes and looking into mine.

"Sure that you're my mate? Darlin', we wouldn't be able to …"

Cutting me off she says, "No. I understand that we're mates. I can feel the pull to you. In that memory you just shared I could feel how happy you were. I want to know how you can be so sure I'll make you happy. We don't even know each other, Pike."

"Bloom, you were made for me. We have one person out there who was put here just for us and you are mine and I'm yours. That's the way of our kind. We may not know everything about each other yet, but we will. And the more we learn the stronger our bond will become." I grab her hand and pull her closer placing it over my heart and I tell her, "The moment I caught your scent I knew I'd found you. This place in my chest, that's felt incomplete for so long, finally feels whole again and it's because I found my mate."

She closed her eyes at my words and I know she's taking in each beat of my heart under her finger tips. I set there for what feels like hours with her hand pressed against my heart until she finally breaks the silence.

"I was falling to pieces. I was trying so hard to get over losing my Dad, but I wasn't succeeding. I had pushed Bonnie and Billy away. I wanted nothing but to cover my head and stay in the darkness that my life had become. Then I found you and the hole in my chest started to heal. After a year of crying over the loss of my father, I finally started feeling whole again. You saved me twice this week, from Trace and from myself."

Before the first tear can break through her eyelashes, I throw my arms around her and press her tight to my chest.

"We saved each other, darlin'. I was running from my past, from my future and you saved me. You gave me direction when I was running aimlessly." Not wanting to keep anything from her I send her the memory of taking out my own father. I don't want to scare her but I need her to see how much pain I was in before I found her.

Gripping me tighter she cries for me and the hard choice I was forced to make and I cry for the loss of her father. A man I'll never meet, but love all the same because he gave me her.

When I know she's cried her last tear I ask, "Are you going to be okay, darlin'?"

She looks up into my face and smiles, "Yeah, I think we both will be just fine, Tennessee."

I smile at her nickname for me then offer to fix her lunch. She slept through breakfast because of her injuries from last night, so I'm certain she's hungry, but she declines my offer to cook and insists on doing it herself. When she gets up to go to the kitchen I ask to borrow her phone to contact the pack.

I dial Emily first and pray that she answers even though she won't recognize the number.

"Hello?" she asks questioningly

"Em, it's me."

"Pike, oh my gosh! Where are you?"

"Ohio."

"You ran all the way to Ohio? What the heck were you thinking big brother?" Emily scolds me.

"It's fine. Better than fine. I found her, Em."

"Found who?" She asks confused.

"My mate." I have to pull the phone back from my ear when she starts to whoop and holler.

When she settles down she starts firing questions at me, "When are you coming home? Can I come there to meet her? What's her name? What's she like? Can I call her my sister?"

Chuckling at her enthusiasm I answer all her questions in order, "We're still discussing it, but I think we'll be heading home sometime this week. You don't need to come here to meet her because we're coming there. Her name is Bloom. She's amazing. And you'll have to ask her the last question."

"I'm so happy for you, big brother. I can't wait to meet her. Everyone is going to be so excited."

"Em, you have to keep this secret for now."

"Why? It's great news."

"I know it is, but there's something going on that's hard to explain over the phone. I'll have to handle it when I get there, just promise me you won't tell anyone where I am or about my mate. Please sis, I need this from you."

"Of course, Pike. You can trust me, just hurry home. I want to meet my new sister."

"We will. Love you, Em. Be careful. I have to call Tucker now and check in."

"Love you too, brother. Be careful yourself," she replies before hanging up.

I quickly call Tucker and relay the same information to him and (other than the girlie squeals) got the same reaction from him that I got from Emily. He catches me up on the pack and I'm thankful to hear everything has been running smooth. Then I ask him to overnight me some items I need. I need my own clothes and money. The hardest thing about shifting is not being able to carry my must have items with me. He promises to ship the stuff out right away and then we both say goodbye.

By the time I finish with my calls Bloom has finished lunch, so I go in the kitchen to join her.

Finishing off my third hamburger I tell her, "Thanks, darlin', that really hit the spot."

Trailing her finger around the rim of her glass of sweet tea she looks up at me and smiles, "You're welcome, Tennessee."

"Speaking of Tennessee …."

"I know you need to get back." Her finger pauses on the glass as she closes her eyes and takes a deep breath then lets it out before saying, "I'll go with you."

I release the breath I was holding in. "Thanks, for not fighting me on this. They need me there. I promise you'll love it." I'm so pleased that she isn't saying no.

"But I want Bonnie to come with me." She announces her ultimatum. I know those two are as thick as thieves but Bonnie has a life here how can she possibly pack up her life and follow us.

"I can hear your thoughts now, Tennessee," she reminds me with a smug grin.

"Sorry. Do you think Bonnie will be able to pack up and move away from her family?" I ask.

"I don't know, but I hope so because I'd like to have a familiar face there to help me through this. It's going to be a big change, Pike. I've never lived anywhere but here. My Dad built this house," she says looking around the room clearly taking in all the memories that cling there.

"We'll come back and visit. You can keep your house and we'll use it as a vacation home. I bet Billy will keep a good eye on it for ya."

"That might work, but I'd still like to ask Bonnie to come along, if you don't mind."

"Darlin', if it makes you happy it makes me happy," I say grabbing her hand that's been fiddling with her glass of tea.

"Thank you," she whispers as she watches our joined hands.

I help her clear the table then follow her into the living room where we snuggle up on the couch. We plan on watching a movie but in the decision process we get caught up in learning each other's favorite things.

"What's your favorite movie?" I ask tracing my fingers up her neck to her hairline then back down her shoulder.

"Anything with John Wayne," she answers as a shiver races down her body from my touch.

"Oh a western fan. I like that." I smile at the back of her head.

"What about you, Tennessee?"

"Promise you won't laugh?"

"Spit it out," she pushes.

"The Notebook," I mumble.

Turning around and looking me in the face she asks trying to hold in a laugh, "Did you just say The Notebook?"

"Yes," I grumble.

"As in the best chick flick ever, two hour long epic love story, kissing in the rain, Nicholas Sparks The Notebook?"

"Yes, that very movie, and I'm secure enough in my man hood to say I cry every time I watch it," I say puffing out my chest.

"Good choice." She giggles.

"Darlin'?" I ask pulling her giggling self back into my arms.

"Hmm?" She manages after she finally calms down.

"Promise me you'll never tell the guys in the pack I just admitted that. As far as they know their Alpha loves movies with fast cars and explosions."

"It's our dirty little secret, Tennessee."

Chapter 22 – Bloom

~ Lusty Threats ~

It feels so right to be wrapped up in his arms, I guess if I believe everything he's telling me then I'm made to be here. And if I'm being truthful with myself I believe he's right about us being mates. Even though I've just met him, I feel as if I can trust him with my life. If you can't trust the shifter put on this earth for you, who can you trust?

Curled up together we learn we have some things in common, like our love of country music and classic muscle cars. As well as some things we'll probably never see eye to eye on, he loves pineapple on his pizza while I stick with the classic pepperoni. When he asks me my favorite color his eyes pop into my mind and I automatically blurt out ocean blue, which causes my cheeks to turn ten shades of red. He rewards my honesty with a kiss on the top of my head and I can see in his mind that his favorite color now comes from my hazel eyes, which puts a smile on my face the rest of the afternoon. I'm surprised by how easily I can now pick up on his thoughts. Our conversation has an easy give and take, but on the rare occasion one of us is embarrassed or nervous about our answer the other easily picks the answer out of the others thoughts. Pike explains to me that after the mating is complete and with enough practice we'll be able to access all of each other's memories. I'm nervous about him seeing the dark place I was in this past year, but when that thought crosses my mind he pulls me closer and reassures me that he's here for me now. As nervous as I am I also realize I'm excited to be able to see his life growing up in a pack.

When the sun sets we figure it's time to get up and make dinner. He takes my hand and pulls me to my feet and keeps a hold of it while we walk the short distance into the kitchen only releasing it so I can search the cabinets for something to make us.

"How does spaghetti sound?" I ask looking at him around the edge of the cabinet door.

"It sounds perfect like you, darlin'," he replies from the perch he's taken on the counter.

"Pike, I'm far from perfect," I sigh hiding my face back behind the door under the pretense of gathering the cooking supplies. I hear him hop down seconds before I feel his arms wrap around my waist.

His lips pressed to my ear and he whispers, "In my opinion you're perfect and anyone that disagrees will have to answer to me." Moving his mouth farther down to the crook in my neck he breathes, "Though you should know this little freckle right here might be the reason you are so perfect." Then he takes my breath away by planting those deliciously kissable lips right on that freckle. I grab the counter in front of me and slam my eyes closed, praying for him to only move those lips if he's going to take them from my neck to put them on my mouth, and for the first time since this madness began I thank the lord he can read my thoughts because he spins me around and gives me exactly what I was been praying for.

He starts gently but when I throw my arms around his neck digging my fingers into his raven hair his lips become demanding and I part my lips so he can join his tongue with mine. We can't get close enough, can't get enough, and in that moment I feel fairly certain I'll never be able to get enough of this man in my arms. His kisses taste sweeter than hot chocolate, chocolate chip cookies, and hot fudge sundaes combined.

I knew he'd taste delicious. My wolf sure is a know it all. Geez!

When he pulls back to catch his breath I want to drag him back to soothe the ache I feel from the loss of his body against mine. He chuckles at my thoughts as he runs his hand through his hair then leans in to place one more chaste kiss on my lips before saying,

"You've already had a rough 24 hours and you need more time to process everything that's happened before we go further."

"We're just kissing." I cross my arms over my chest and look down, my chin on my chest, my lips pouted.

Putting his hand under my chin he tilts my head back so he can look into my eyes, "Darlin', if we keep kissing like that I won't be able to stop myself from draggin' you into your bedroom and …"

"Alright, point taken," I cut him off by pulling my chin out of his grasp so he can't see the blush that I know has inevitably covered my checks.

"Bloom, are you a …" he starts to ask.

"We are not having this conversation, Pike," I cut him off again.

His scans my face for a few seconds and I'm convinced he'll push the topic, but finally he backs up and says, "I'll drop it for now, darlin', but only because I'm starving."

Letting out a sigh I turn back to the cabinet to finish gathering the ingredients for dinner. I hear him pull out a chair at the table and know he's sat down, so I begin going through my mental list of everything needed for the spaghetti. When I reach up high to grab the box of pasta he makes me jump by stating, "Oh Bloom, just so you know I *will* be getting the answer to my question one way or another."

His declaration causes my pulse to race and I take a moment to compose myself before I turn to face him. He has his legs stretched out in front of him crossed at the ankles and his arms stuck behind his head and a wolfish grin plastered to his face. Cocking one eyebrow and sticking my hand on my hip I ask, "Do you really want to tick off the person cooking your dinner? I could easily slip some chocolate into yours and where would your furry behind be?"

"I'm not a dog!" He throws his hands in the air in exasperation.

I ignore his outburst at my threat and set out to make our dinner. He watches my every move without saying a word and it's sending shivers of pleasure down my body. By the time the food's finished cooking, I'm squirming under his gaze and I can see the hint of smile on his face and I want to smack it off there. Just because we're mates doesn't mean he needs to ravish my thoughts. Crossing over to the table I throw the plate down in front of him more than ready to give him a mouthful for tormenting me after *he* stopped us earlier, but the sight of the spaghetti flying into his lap causes me to disintegrate into a fit of giggles. He pulls me into his lap and takes my plate and dumps it on my head. The next thing I know we're running around the kitchen throwing pasta back in forth like snowballs. I try to run past him to get out of the room and into the bathroom but he catches me around the waist and pulls me tight against his chest. Leaning in he licks some sauce off my neck and says, "Delicious, if none survived the fight I'll be more than happy to lick my dinner off your body."

I suck in a breath at the heat in his eyes and the thoughts that are running through his mind. He's leaning in to follow through on his lusty threat when he stops to sniff the air. His head turns toward the front door just as a knock rings through the house and he lets go of my waist.

In six long strides he crosses the living room and jerks the door open and engulfs the person on the other side in a back breaking hug. When he releases the person I hear him ask, "What are you doing here? I told you we'd be home in a few days."

I'm surprised by the silvery voice that answers, "I couldn't wait any longer, Pike. I missed you."

Oh heck no! You better get in there and stake our claim. My jealousy (and my bossy wolf) pushes me forward to find out who's talking to my mate in such a loving way and I use all my weight to push Pike out of the way to get a look. There on my porch stands the most beautiful woman I've ever seen and that includes on TV. She has to be pushing 6 feet tall with lean, muscular arms and legs that seem to go for miles. Her hair is black as night and pin straight falling just below her chin in choppy layers. Then there are those eyes, the color of the clearest blue ocean, the same as Pikes. The realization hits me and pulls back mine and my wolf's need to stake our claim just as Pike introduces us.

"Bloom, this is my baby sister Emily." Then he puts his arm around my waist and pulls me to his side, "Em, this is my mate Bloom Daniels." I wait as she sizes me up just like I'd done her, but unlike the beauty in front of me I'm embarrassed. It's not that I don't see myself as beautiful but being covered from head to toe in spaghetti will make anyone feel like a troll next to this goddess. A smile crosses her face and softens her angular features then she pulls me into bone crushing hug that can easily rival the one her brother had given her moments before.

"Gracious, I'm so excited to meet you," she whispers into my ear then pulling back asks, "Can I come in? I wasn't interrupting anything was I?"

Moving out of the way to let her in the door, "Of course not, please, come in."

Stepping in she looks at her brother and says, "Pike, will you go grab my bags out of the rental car. I brought the things you asked Tuck to send too."

He kisses her cheek, gives me a wink and then walks out to the car leaving us alone. I offer her a seat and ask if she wants something to drink, which she declines and then when Pike walks back in I excuse myself so I can take a shower and change out of my Spaghetti covered clothes.

Chapter 23 – Pike

~ I'll cross that bridge when I get to it ~

I watch Bloom as she walks out of the room then when I hear the bathroom door click shut I turn to Emily.

"I've missed you, little sister."

"I've missed you too, big brother. Now tell me why you didn't want the pack to know you found your mate." That's my sister; she's never been one to beat around the bush.

"Does she smell like a wolf to you?"

"Pike, the pack isn't going to care if you mated with a human as long as she's your real mate."

"She's not human, well at least not fully," I say and then watched as her face draws up in confusion.

"Explain, how is she not human?" She demands.

I look at the hall Bloom had disappeared down and listen for the water, when I'm certain she won't be able to hear our conversation I continue.

"Her mother's a shifter and her father was a human."

"Then, why don't I smell her wolf side?" Emily cocks her head to the side and asks.

"She's never shifted, though I can say she does heal fast like we do."

"Okay, that has to be a first, but I still don't see why you're keeping this a secret."

Letting out a sigh I brace myself for the revelation I'm getting ready to lay on my little sister. "Her mother left when she was a new born, so up until this morning Bloom never knew about her wolf side.

Apparently, Bloom's father wasn't her mother's mate and not long after delivering Bloom she ran into her real mate and left with him. She hasn't been in her life since then."

Sympathy showing in her eyes Emily looks toward the hall and I can see her need to go comfort my mate over the loss of her mother at a young age. When she turns her gaze back to me I see the unshed tears in her eyes and she asks, "Does she even know who her mother is?"

"She's seen pictures and her father has told her about her mother, but he didn't know about her wolf side either."

"Why would she hide that from a person she loved? This woman is sounding more and more selfish as this story goes on. If I knew where she was I'd go smack the heck out of her," she grumbles pacing the room.

"That's the thing, Em, we do know her," I finally confess as I collapse on the couch from the weight of my revelation.

Emily stops pacing and looks me square in the eyes. She doesn't have to even ask I know she wants the womans name and I can no longer keep it to myself.

"Rose O'Brian."

"Tuckers mom?" She gasps in surprise.

I nod then watched as she crosses the room and collapses on the couch next to me. We set like that in silence for several minutes then looking up at the ceiling she asks, "Have you told her you know her mom? Hell, have you told Tucker that him and the twins have a sister?"

"Nope."

She punches me hard in my arm and demands, "Why not?"

"Because if I tell her that her long lost mother is part of our pack back home she won't want to come back with me." I sigh.

"And how do you think she's going to feel when she finds out you lied to her, dork," Emily demands turning to stare at my face.

"I'll cross that bridge when I get to it; right now I need to get her home." Lying to my mate is eating me up inside and I want to tell her the truth, but what if she refuses to go with me because Rose is there. I can't leave my pack without their Alpha much longer, and there's no way I'm leaving my mate. Even if she hadn't been attacked last night, I can't leave half my heart in Ohio. I know it makes me selfish, but at this point I don't care.

Changing the subject I ask, "So how did you get here so fast?"

She watches me while she deliberates on pushing the subject of me telling Bloom then her shoulders slump and she falls back into the couch and I know she's made her decision. "Just so you know, I don't like that we're keeping this from her. She deserves to know what we're dragging her into Pike."

"I know Em, but right now I feel like my hands are tied." We set there staring at nothing in particular for several minutes then Emily sighs.

"I hopped the first plane to Columbus, then rented the car and drove the rest of the way down here."

"I suppose Tucker told you the address?" I ask thankful she drops the previous subject, for now.

"Yeah, he wanted to come too but he knew he couldn't leave the command you left him. I guess with this new discovery it's good that he didn't."

"Yeah, it is. So what'd you bring me?"

Waving her hand towards the simple green duffle bag I carried in with her ridiculously expensive designer luggage she says, "A couple outfits, those nasty boots you love so much, your wallet, deodorant, toothbrush, and your cell. You said you'd be coming home in a few days so I didn't think you'd need much else. If I forgot anything you have your money now so you'll be able to replace it."

"Thanks, I need a good shower and my own clothes."

Looking over at me and taking in my spaghetti covered borrowed sweats she asks, "Whose are you wearing anyways?"

"This guy Billy, he was a friend of Bloom's Dad. He knows about us from Rose."

She opens her mouth to respond to the fact that Rose revealed her true self to Billy and not Michael, but quickly closes her mouth and shakes her head from side to side. I have a feeling when we get home, Bloom won't be facing her long lost mother alone. Emily's loyalty has already latched it's self onto Bloom and once Em decides something it would be easier to rip her arm off than try to get her to change her mind.

Just then Bloom walks back into the living room rubbing the towel over her hair. She looks at Em then back at me and says, "I left you some hot water. After you're done I thought maybe we could go to Billy's and get a pizza, if you're still hungry that is."

I stand up and cross the room to stand directly in front of her. She tilts her head up to look into my eyes and I see the desire staring back at me. Just being close is driving us both crazy with need, but I won't do anything to embarrass her in front of my sister so instead of pulling her the last few inches to my body, like my wolf is howling for me to do, I simply place one of my hands on her neck and use my thumb to rub circles over the freckle there. When her eyes flutter close and a soft moan escapes her lips I grin and say, "Pizza sounds great, you'll learn quickly that us wolves have a very high metabolism so it takes a lot to fill us up." Pulling away from her and grabbing the duffle bag Emily brought me, I head towards the bathroom but before I'm out of ear shot I add, "and a lot to tire us out too, darlin'."

I hear her sharp intake of breath and her heart rate speed up and I know my meaning got through. I don't think the grin on my face can go any wider as I take in the thoughts running through my mate's mind.

Chapter 24 – Bloom

~ I'm a freaking Alpha? ~

"I know we just met, but I'd like for you to feel comfortable with me. We're going to be related, so if you have any questions please feel free to ask me." Emily says breaking into my thoughts. We came into the kitchen to straighten up while Pike takes his shower.

Wiping down the counter I have a hundred questions running through my mind. Finally I pick out the one that's at the front most of my thoughts.

"Will you explain this mating thing to me? I understand that Pike and I are mates. I feel the pull to him and when we try we can read each other thoughts but is there more to it? Is there something we have to do to cement this bond?"

She smiles at me from the sink, "Yes, your bond's already recognized each other, but the mating won't be complete till Pike marks you as his and introduces you as such in front of the pack. We usually hold a ceremony a lot like a wedding to do this. At the ceremony he'll announce you as his mate and the two of you will make a pledge to each other, then you will spend some time at a reception so the whole pack can congratulate you, then the two of you'll leave and that night he'll mark you as his."

Confusion clearly showing on my face I ask, "How does he mark me?"

"Well he bites you, usually in a place everyone can see like your neck or shoulder. The bite heals fast but it leaves a scar. It's the shifter's version of a wedding ring." She explains watching my face to see my reaction.

"H-h-h-he has to b-b-bite me!" I stutter turning my face away to hide the blush that's covered my cheeks.

The thought of Pike sinking his teeth into the same spot on my neck where he kissed me less than an hour ago sends shivers through my body. My body's craving Pike's mark, which is confusing and exciting me all at the same time. I'm not sure I'll ever get use to these feelings he causes me to have. Heck, that kiss earlier had me putty in his arms.

"Don't be embarrassed, Bloom, the bite is a very normal thing in our culture. I've been told it's very pleasurable." That's what I'm afraid of, ugh.

"You haven't found your mate?" I ask turning back to look at her.

A wistful look crosses her face when she says, "Not yet. We don't usually find them until we're in our mid-twenties and I'm only 21. So I have a few more years."

"But, I'm only 20."

"Yes, but your mate is 25 and I think your bond knew you two needed each other sooner."

I think about the dark place I went into after losing Dad and then of Pike running after having to take out his father and realize that Emily's right; we needed each other.

"Any other questions?" she asks going back to the dishes.

"I have hundreds," I answer honestly.

"Well, then we better get started or we'll be here all night." She giggles.

"Okay, will you tell me how the pack works? I know Pike is now the Alpha, but that's about it."

"Well, there's also his beta, Tucker. Beta is the second-in-command after the Alpha pair. Then there are the pack elders, they don't have as much control as the Alpha or the Beta but they are respected. The Alpha usually uses them as council. There is usually an Omega in a pack, as well. They're outside of the pack hierarchy and have the ability to calm the members of the pack. But, our pack hasn't had one since my momma died." She gets quiet after mentioning her mom and I know she needs the moment to remember her so I don't push her to go on. She grabs a dishtowel and wipes her eyes then continues. "As Pike's mate, you'll be the female Alpha. Any problems among the women will go through you first. If you feel you need Pike's help you can bring him into the problems as well. The rest of the pack is ranked by strength. And of course the male and female rankings are separate."

"I'm going to be in charge of a group of wolf women? Emily, I can't even shift!"

"Bloom, you may not shift but I can feel your strength. My wolf recognizes you as her Alpha." If my wolf was a cat she would've been purring at that proclamation. She likes the idea of being in charge of a bunch of she-wolves.

I'm a freaking Alpha? *Of course, we're an alpha!* Don't wolves fight for their dominance? *Well we sure don't settle it by taking a vote.* "What if someone challenges me? That's how these rankings work, right? I can't shift so I'll be fighting them as human!" I say dropping the rag I'm using to wipe down the mess.

Emily wipes her wet hands off on the towel and then comes over to me and places a hand on each of my arms. "Bloom, please calm down. Pack members don't challenge the Alphas, because as Alpha they carry the strength of the entire pack in them." Wow, that isn't helping. I don't want to carry the strength of a pack of wolves in me. Dang it, I have a hard enough time carrying around my own freaking problems let alone all of theirs.

"Darlin', you won't be carrying the burden alone. I will be right beside you, so please don't stress your pretty little self," Pike says pulling my attention to him. His black hair is damp and it makes his already impossibly dark hair even darker. A simple white t-shirt clings to his muscular chest, a pair of dark blue boot cut jeans hang low on his hips and worn in black work boots cover his feet. The whole look makes for a mouth watering package. The smirk that covers his face tells me that he's reading my thoughts and is taking great pleasure in it. To tease him I send him the image of him marking my neck and then turn around and continue talking to Emily.

"So I think we're done cleaning up in here. Thanks for helping."

"You're welcome. So are we getting pizza?" She asks smiling as she looks back and forth between Pike and me.

"Go outside now, Emily," Pike growls from behind me.

Laughing she walks out of the room leaving me alone with her brother. He waits until he hears the door slam and then he swings me around and lifts me up into his arms. My traitorous body nuzzles closer to him and I bury my face into his neck.

"I see Emily told you about sealing our mating bond." His voice still sounds more wolf than human and it's causing butterflies to form in my stomach. My own voice seems to have disappeared so I nod my head against his neck.

Bending his head he nuzzles into my own neck and whispers, "I wish I could mark you now, darlin'. It's taking all my control not to, so please no more teasing me like that. I'm not sure I'll be able to hold off if you keep sending me thoughts like that. Okay?"

"Okay," I manage to agree as he places me back on the floor in front of him.

Leaning in he places a chaste kiss on my lips then grabs my hand, "Okay, sugar, let's go get some grub."

Billy's is packed but we find a booth in the back of the dining room that gives us some privacy. We put in our drink order and I ask the waitress to send Billy out, he comes out promptly carrying a tray with our drinks. After setting them in front of us he scoots into the booth beside Emily and introduces himself. Then turning his attention to me and Pike says, "I spoke with Jim earlier and he said Bonnie's car was at his office when he got to work this morning. One of your friends must have been nice enough to bring it back from the lake last night after the accident."

Trace had taken Bonnie's car last night after he attacked me, so it must have been him that dropped it off. But I'm not about to tell Billy that because he doesn't know Trace attacked me and I'd like to keep it that way.

"That was nice of them," Pike says going along with it.

"And he said that Bonnie and he dropped Trace's back at his place, but he wasn't there. But I still don't understand why Bonnie had Trace's vehicle instead of her own." He looks between the two of us waiting for one of us to blurt out the truth. He's always been able to tell when I'm not telling him the full truth, but this time I'm not backing down. He's had to worry about me enough this past year I don't want to add this on top of it.

"Bonnie told you that her car was blocked in so Trace let her borrow his jeep," Pike tries to explain.

"Okay, but how did she know about the wreck." Billy continues with his interrogation. I can tell by the set of his shoulders he isn't planning on giving up until we confess the truth. But thankfully I have a stubborn wolf beside me who apparently isn't planning on giving in either.

"Billy, we went over all of this last night and honestly I think we're tired of talking about it. It's been a stressful 24 hours for all of us and we should just move on and try to enjoy the rest of this evening. Emily and I are both looking forward to tasting this pizza of yours that Bloom raved about the whole way here." I watch the two of them stare each other down and when Billy slumps back in the booth, I know he's giving up, for the moment.

"You're right, I should be letting you guys enjoy your night. So what would you like on your pizza?" We give him our order and then he gets up and leaves the table. Rubbing Pike's arm I whisper, "Please let me out, I need to go talk to him. He needs to know I'm leaving with you guys."

He scoots out and helps me out. Before I can turn to head to the kitchen he grabs my hand, "Darlin', this isn't goodbye for you and Billy. We'll be back to visit and he's more than welcome to come visit us. So please don't see it that way. I don't want you to think I'm trying to separate you from the people that love you. I just ... I need you with me, Bloom." His confession rocks me on my heels. He needs me. Can't he see I'm the one that needs him?

"I know, Pike. But it's still going to be hard leaving this place. It's always been home." I squeeze his hand reassuringly then release it. "I'll be right back."

The kitchen is busy but I find in Billy in his usual spot making our order personally. I sneak up behind him and wrap my arms around his waist and lay my head on his back. He pats my hand and continues to put the toppings on. "What's wrong, doll?" Of course, he knows it's me behind him. I'm the only one who'd been in his kitchen hugging him like this, we may not be family by blood but we've been family in heart ever since I was born. This man has been there and raised me right along with my father. And now that he's gone, Billy's the only link I have to that part of my life.

I release him and walk to the other side of the counter, "I'm moving to Tennessee." Better to get it over with quick, like a band aid.

"I figured you would," he finishes placing the pepperonis and then starts on the cheese. "So when are you leaving?"

"In a couple of days, but we'll come back to visit and you're more than welcome to come see me there."

"I'd like that, doll. What are you going to do about the cabin?"

"Well, I was hoping you'll keep an eye on it for me. I don't want to sell it and we could stay there when we come back to visit."

"So you're already a *we*?" He asks still focusing on the pizza.

By agreeing to go with Pike to Tennessee I guess I'm also agreeing to become a *we*. The thought frightens the day lights out of me. What does it really mean to be a *we* with an Alpha wolf? Ugh! This is all happening so fast, but I've already committed myself to the move so I won't let my insecurities make me back out on my word.

"Yeah, I guess we are," I answer watching his expression, which is giving nothing away.

He doesn't answer for several minutes while he finishes topping my pizza with extra cheese. I watch him turn and place it in the oven then he turns back to me and says, "Bloom, I'm going to miss you fiercely, but as much as I hate to admit it, I believe this is going to be good for you. That man out there has brought the light back to your eyes and I can't fault him for that. If he can make you happy I won't try to stop you from leaving."

Walking around the counter I throw myself back into his arms, "Billy, I needed you to understand. I love you so much."

He has one arm wrapped around me while the other strokes my hair. "I love you too, Bloom Michael. And I promise I'll be coming to see you. I have to come and make sure those wolves are treating my girl right."

"Like I'd let them treat me any other way," I reply, grinning up at him.

"No, I guess you wouldn't." He releases me then says, "Go back out to your guests so I can finish up your order. Or else I'm gonna put you to work."

Chapter 25 – Pike

~ Right beside my mate ~

My mate wasn't lying when she said Billy's had the best pizza, dang I ate two larges by myself and three slices of his homemade apple pie. Thank goodness my shifter genes give me a fast metabolism or I'd be well over 500 pounds. When we finished, Billy came out and told us all bye, he pulled me aside and told me to keep Bloom safe. Which of course I plan on doing, but I don't need to be rude so I agree I will. He asks if he can visit once we get settled in Tennessee and I let him know he's always welcome. I understand what he is to my mate and like I told her, I don't want to keep her from the people she loves.

On the drive home Emily tells Bloom more about living in a pack and I let myself enjoy the feel of her beside me. Last night I almost lost her to some psycho stalker and the thought rocks me to my core. My wolf wants nothing more but to hunt him down and honestly my human side isn't fighting him on it too much. The only thing stopping me is Bloom. I can't leave her unprotected while I go after revenge. She needs my protection though I doubt she'll admit it and I need to know she's close so my wolf will stay calm. Eventually, we'll be able to be apart but that won't happen till I know Trace is no longer a threat and we're safely back with my pack. I have Tucker tracking Trace down, Bloom figures he's skipped town after what he did last night, but the predator in me knows he hasn't given up. If anything he'll be more determined to get his hands on my mate.

After parking in front of the cabin I get out and pull Bloom out my side of the car, since she's sitting right beside me in the middle. Taking her hand we walk up the steps, unlock the door, step into the living room and then I drop onto the couch pulling her down on top of me. She giggles as she cuddles in closer to me.

Taking a seat in one of the recliners Emily huffs, "You two do realize that I'm super tired and you've taken over my bed for the night, right?"

Bloom props herself up and looks over at Emily, "I wouldn't make you sleep on the couch when there's the spare room now that Billy cleaned out da …" A wistful expression crosses her face for less than a heartbeat as she thinks about her Dad then she clears it away replacing it with a smile and continues, "It's not much but it's just been cleaned and I think he even put new sheets on the bed. So you're more than welcome to use that room while we're here."

"That sounds perfect. Thanks, Blu!" Emily gushes.

"No problem, plus your brother will need the couch to sleep on anyway."

Sliding out from underneath her and standing I snarl, "The hell I am!" She must have lost her mind if she thinks I'll be sleeping on that couch.

She stares up at me stunned for all of two seconds before she rights herself on the couch and flatly asks, "And where the heck do you think you'll be sleeping?"

Crossing my arms over my chest I answer, "Right beside my mate." Where I belong!

Standing she mimics my stance by crossing her arms and staring up at me, "The hell you are. I've never had a man sleep in my bed before and that's not gonna change tonight." Well, I like hearing that no other man's been in her bed, but still, I'm her mate.

"How quick you forget darlin', I've been sleeping beside you all week." I uncross my arms and reach out to place my palm to her cheek.

She pulls back. "That's not the same Pike Masterson and you know it. I thought you were a freaking dog!"

"I am not a dog!" I growl then lifting her up, I throw her over my shoulder. "And I will be sleeping right beside my mate tonight." Emily giggles causing me to remember we have an audience. "Goodnight, little sister. Make sure the doors locked, please. I kind of have my hands full."

Kicking her legs and scratching at my back Bloom demands, "Put me down now!"

"Scratch a little lower, will ya darlin'? I have an itch I can't reach." I chuckle and wink at my sister who laughs at the two of us some more.

"Scratch yourself, you overgrown dog!" She still kicks but stops the scratching.

"I'm not a dog," I correct, swatting her butt which causes her to go still.

"Good gir…" I start to say but I'm stopped short when Bloom hauls back and slams her elbow into the back of my head.

"Don't ever smack my ass again!" She growls then continues to try to wiggle free while I'm stunned. By sure will, I keep her on my shoulder as I head us toward the bedroom.

Emily's laughing so hard I can barely understand her when she calls after us, "Goodnight, big brother. Goodnight, Bloom."

Resigned to her fate, for the moment, Bloom stops kicking and sighs, "Goodnight, Emily."

I kick the door shut with my foot, toss her on the bed and then spread myself out beside her. She jumps up and throws her hands on her hips all the while glaring at me.

"You arrogant, over bearing, pain in my …"

"Now, now darlin', a lady doesn't use that kind of language."

"And a gentleman wouldn't throw a lady around like a sack of potatoes, so you can bite me!"

I arch an eyebrow and a wolfish grin overtakes my face. "My pleasure, mate, just show me where you'd like it." Her cheeks become flamed and I grin wider at the delicious thoughts that are going through her mind. As mad as I may make her, she still wants my mark and I want to see it on her.

I slide to the edge of the bed and grab the loops in her jeans to pull her closer. She drops her hands from her hips but keeps the glare on her face as I circle my arms around her waist and look up at her with puppy dog eyes.

"Oh, I don't think so mister. If you think I'm gonna forgive you just because you mention marking me and give me that look you are sadly mistaken." She tries to remove my arms but I tighten my grip pulling her closer to my chest.

"Darlin', I really am sorry. But I need you to see it my way."

"And what way is that?" She asks crossing her arms in front of her to put some distance between us, once she realizes she isn't getting out of my arms until I decide to let her out.

"Twenty-four hours ago you were attacked and I could've lost you and I haven't ripped the man apart, yet, like my wolf is demanding. So until this threat to your safety is over, I will be glued to your side and if that means I sleep beside you so be it." Though I would've insisted on sleeping beside my mate even if there was no threat.

"Pike, you do remember I can read your thoughts too, right? So I heard that unspoken part." She reminds me looking awful proud of herself for catching me.

"Sorry darlin', but that doesn't change the fact that there is a threat and I'll feel much better if I know I'm in here protecting you."

"Fine, but there will be no funny business. Mate or not, I am not ready for … that." Her cheeks blush a little and I reach up and brush my thumb along the pinkened spot. The fact that I can make her body react to me even in these little ways makes me long for our bonding to be complete so I can have her completely. I won't push her, because I know she's not ready, but someday she will be and I'll take great pleasure in seeing if the rest of her body blushes like her cheeks.

She clears her throat. Dang she must have caught those thoughts as well; I really need to remember to block my mind.

"Umm ... I need to go get changed and brush my teeth." She steps out of my arms and goes to her dresser and pulls out some night clothes. She turns to me before heading out the door. "You can get changed in here. I promise to knock before I come back in." Then she slips out the door shutting it behind her.

I don't think she'd like it if I sleep in my boxers so I grab my bag out of the living room and find a pair of pajama bottoms Emily packed me. I strip down then pull them on and decide to go without a shirt. I can handle the pants but I know a shirt will get tangled in the sheets and make me uncomfortable, plus without it I have a good chance of feeling my mates hands against my bare chest. Climbing into the bed I make myself comfortable as I wait on her to join me. She's dressed and has brushed her teeth but I can hear her giving herself a pep talk and it makes me smile.

Come on Bloom, you can do this. It's Pike, your mate ... your very attractive mate. You're just going to sleep beside him, nothing else. You both will have clothes on. Oh crap, what if he sleeps naked? No, he wouldn't do that. Would he? Ugh! Alright suck it up. He's probably listening to this little rant and laughing at you.

"Pike?"

"Sorry darlin', I can't help myself. You are pretty darn adorable when you're flustered. If it helps put you at ease, I promise I have pants on."

"That does help, a little. I'll be right there."

The door opens slowly and she steps in then closes it back. She has on white cotton sleep shorts that have popsicles printed on them and a red racer back tank top and I have to say it may be the sexiest thing I have ever seen. I push the cover back from her side and pat the spot on the bed beside me. She climbs in and I don't hesitate pulling her into my arms so her head lies against my bare chest. To my surprise she relaxes, letting out a contented sigh as she tangles our legs together so we'll be closer.

"Tennessee?" I love when she calls me that.

"Yes, darlin'?"

"Will you tell me what it's like to be a wolf?"

Her question shocks me and I lean back so I can look at her face, something isn't right. "What's wrong?"

She waited a few moments then says, "I keep wondering why I never shifted. From what you and Emily have told me, I definitely should have and now that I know that I feel like I'm mourning the loss of a huge part of myself."

"Your wolf." I run my fingers through her hair pushing it away from her face.

"Exactly! Today, I started realizing that there is another side to me, my wolf side, and she's probably always been there making me stronger and protecting me. I just never gave her any notice, but now I really want to know why she never came out. Why can't I shift?"

"I'd like to know that too, darlin', and I promise as soon as we get home we'll talk to the Elders. One of them should be able to help us figure out what's keeping her in."

"Thank you." She lightly kisses my chest and says, "Good night, Tennessee."

I kiss the top of her head. "Good night, darlin'."

Chapter 26 – Bloom

~ Till the good lord pulls the last breath from my body ~

When I wake up I find myself tangled around Pike. It feels so right to be there and I'm not ready to move yet so I snuggle back in and lay my head back against his chest. His unique scent surrounds me like a favorite blanket and I sigh at the familiarity. I can't believe how much my life has changed in the past week. I've gone from being so depressed I can barely get out of bed or stop crying to not wanting to get out of bed because I'm content wrapped in the arms of my half man/half wolf mate.

"Half man/half wolf?" Pike grumbles still half asleep.

"I can't think of a better way to say it. How are you so in tune to my thoughts while you're asleep?" I playfully poke his side.

"Shifter or just plain wolf, would work darlin'. My wolf keeps an eye on you even when I'm asleep. He has to make sure you're safe," he explains then kisses the top of my head.

"Tell him to relax, he needs to sleep too."

"He's a supernatural being, darlin', as long as I get sleep he doesn't have to."

"Interesting," I reply honestly.

"So what do you have planned for us today?" Pike asks as he stretches his arms over his head. I feel the loss of his touch and my wolf screams for me to pull him back to us. Instead of listening to her I roll out of bed and grab my robe.

"Well, Bonnie's coming over and I need to talk to her about going with us. Then I'll probably start packing."

He props himself up on his side and watches me for several moments. "Are you going to be okay if Bonnie says no to going?"

"She'll say yes." I hope.

"But say she doesn't." He's still watching me closely. I can tell he's worried what my answer will be so to reassure him I climb back into bed and set on my knees beside him. Placing my hands on each side of his face I look him in the eyes. It's a dominant move but Emily told me that as his mate, and apparently an alpha in my own right, I have the right to look him in the eyes this way. She also said anyone else who tries will be dealt with, I'm not sure what that means but I'm not ready for the answer so I didn't ask.

"Pike, I said I'm going. So if you're worried I'll back out because she doesn't go then stop. If I give my word I keep it."

He places his hands over mine to pull them away from his face, takes them to his mouth and gently kisses each palm. "That's a big worry off my shoulders, darlin'. I need you with me." I've been wanted before, I've even had people say they needed me before, but those times mean nothing compared to this lethal Alpha wolf whispering it to me like a prayer. He could snap a man's neck like a twig and has a whole pack at his beck and call, yet he needed me, and I can tell he believes it. Hell, I believe it because I know how much I need him.

He releases my hands and sits up the rest of the way so he can press his lips to mine. The kiss is gentle, more about showing our feelings for each other than demanding what we want. I trail my finger tips along his jaw and enjoy the rough feeling of the stubble there. He caresses the crook of my neck with one hand while the other is fisted into the back of my tank top.

A knock on the door causes us to jump apart. We haven't done anything wrong but dang if we don't look guilty at the moment.

"Bloom, someone just pulled in," Emily speaks through the door.

"I'll be right there," I answer back not taking my eyes off of Pike. I lean in and kiss his lips one more time then climb off the bed. He gets up also and heads toward the door.

"Go get ready darlin', I'll see who's here."

"I won't take long. It's probably Bonnie; she said she'd be over early."

He sniffs the air then smiles, "Yep, it's her."

"Seriously Tennessee, that is just wrong. If you don't want me to start cracking jokes then stop acting like a freaking coon dog."

"It can help me keep you safe, so I won't be stopping, but don't worry darlin' you'll get use to my wolfish ways." He winks at me then walks out the door closing it behind him. There seems to be a lot of things I'll have to get use to; his enhanced sense of smell is just the tip of a very large iceberg that's quickly crashing into my life. I figure I'll have to wait and see if I can survive the changes or not. Though I can honestly say I'm darn determined to make it work.

"Iceberg?" Pike asks cutting into my thoughts.

"Yes, an iceberg. I think it sounds like a good example, if you're going to question my inner rants you know you can pull yourself right on out of my thoughts," I snap at him.

"Calm down, darlin', I'm not questioning your rant. I think it's a cute description."

"Uh-huh. Is there a reason you broke into my mind, Tennessee."

"I just want to reassure you that you'll survive the changes and I'm glad to hear you want this to work, though there isn't really a question whether it will or not. We're mates, which makes us perfect for one another."

"I'll try to take your word on it, but I'm the type that has to see it to believe it Pike."

"That sounds like a challenge, darlin'."

"Not a challenge, just the way I am."

"Oh no, it was a challenge and now I'm determined to prove it to ya."

I can practically hear the wheels turning in his mind as he's formulating his plan to win our so called challenge.

"So are you keeping Bonnie company while you talk to me or are you ignoring my friend?" I ask figuring it best to change the subject.

If I keep going on about him proving stuff to me he'll be back in the bedroom to start doing just that.

"Emily and her are talking. They don't even realize I'm not in the conversation."

"Are they getting along?"

"Oh yeah, they keep going on about shoes or something. If I didn't know better I'd say they've been friends forever."

I should've known, Bonnie's never met a stranger and in the few hours I've known Emily she seems the same way.

"That's good to here. If Bonnie agrees to go with us they'll be seeing a lot of each other."

"Yeah they will. Emily's offered to make breakfast. Is French Toast okay with you?"

"Yes, that's my favorite."

"Good, hurry up and get ready, so you can join us."

"Alright, I'll make it quick. Save me some, Tennessee."

"Of course I will, darlin'."

Twenty minutes later I'm freshly showered and dressed in a pair of jean shorts and an old Cincinnati Reds t-shirt. I find Pike and Bonnie sitting at the kitchen table eating while Emily's at the stove making French toast. I take a seat and tell Bonnie and Emily good morning.

"So I hear I'm invited to go to Tennessee with ya," Bonnie says after swallowing a mouthful of food.

Glaring at Pike I answer, "Yes, you are. I planned on talking to you about it myself."

"Sorry, it just popped out." Pike shrugs, a grin on his face as he continues eating his breakfast watching me and Bonnie.

Turning my attention back to my best friend, "So what do you think, Bon?"

"Living in a town full of men who can shift into wolves? Sounds like an adventure, and you know I'm always up for that." I jump up and hug her.

"Thank you, Bon!"

"It's not problem, Blu. The only thing I need to know is where I'm going to live and work." She says hugging me back. I sit back down and look over at

Pike for the answer. He takes a drink of milk to wash down his food then replies, "We'll set you up with an apartment in the pack house and I'll make a couple calls about finding you a job. I know a couple people have been in need of some office help."

"Pack house?" Bonnie and I both ask in unison.

Emily walks over carrying a plate full of French toast, which she sets in the middle of the table before sitting down to make herself a plate. She looks at me and orders, "Make yourself a plate, doll. You'll need the energy for all the packing we're gonna do today." She stares me down as I try to ignore her while I wait on one of them to answer our question.

Giving in I sigh and grab an empty plate and place two pieces on it then pouring syrup over the top ask again, "Okay, what is the pack house?"

She waits till I take my first bite then answers, "It's where the alpha and his family live. It's big enough that any pack member who wants or needs to can live there as well. There are a couple wings of the house that's set up with apartments, most of the top ranking members that are still single live there. The mated pairs usually choose to live outside of the pack house, either on the pack owned land or near town."

Stunned I look between Pike and her and ask, "How big is this place?"

"Big enough for what we need it for," Pike answers simply.

"Alright. Where will I be living?"

Pike raises his eyebrows at my question. "You'll be with your mate, of course." I should've known the answer but I thought I'd double check.

"The pack house is also where we have all pack meetings and mating ceremonies and such. It really is a beautiful place, Bloom." Emily continues explaining even though I'm not listening because Pike picks this moment to talk to me through our bond.

"Are you ok with living with me, darlin'?"

"Yes, but I wish you would've asked instead of taking away my choice," I grumble.

"I'm sorry, but I'll probably do that a lot; it's the wolf in me. He knows what he wants and if he thinks it's good for his mate he will act on it without asking your opinion. I'll try to keep him in check and ask your opinion on things that involve us."

"You better or you and your wolf will find your butts sleeping on the couch, Tennessee."

He chuckles at my threat then pulls out of my thoughts. Bonnie and Emily are still discussing the move so I focus on finishing my breakfast. I can see out the window that it's a clear sunny day and I know I want to slip away for a few hours by myself. If I'm going to be leaving this town for awhile I need to visit Dad's grave to say goodbye. I haven't been there since the funeral because I wasn't strong enough, but now that Pike is here supporting me I know I can handle going.

It takes us most of the day to pack all the things I plan on taking with me, we don't have to worry about the furniture or any of the kitchen items, but we gather all of my clothes, the pictures off the walls, my collection of books and Dads movie collection. Bonnie asks if I want to pack any of Dad's or Rose's stuff from the shed out back, but I know there isn't anything there that will make me feel connected to Dad, just his old clothes. As for Rose's stuff, it could be used to start a bonfire and I wouldn't blink.

The only thing I know without a doubt I won't go without is the swing off the front porch, Dad crafted it with his own hands and he used it to rock me to sleep when I was a baby. When I got older he'd take me out there to read me my bedtime story. Some kids got quiet stuffy rooms with creaking rocking chairs, but my Daddy gave me a warm breeze to gently sway us and the sound of crickets as the background music to our fairytales. Now that I'm older it's where I go to think, and even if I have to make Tennessee build a porch on that humungous pack house, it's coming with us and will be put up.

Taping down a flap on the last box Emily asks, "Since we're done here, do you need help packing, Bonnie?"

"Good heavens yes!"

"You guys go ahead over and I'll meet you there after I run an errand," I tell them.

"Don't even think you're going somewhere without me, darlin'," Pike warns.

"I don't need protecting, Tennessee," I reply taking our conversation into our minds.

"We've went over this, until the threat to you is eliminated I will be stuck to your side like glue. Go ahead and let that sink in so you can get over it and then we can proceed to the grave yard so you can visit with your Daddy."

"H-how?" I could've sworn I've been blocking my thoughts when I was deciding to go to Daddy's grave.

"Nope, we'll have to work on you blocking yourself, but if I'm gonna be honest with ya, darlin', I love knowing I can slip into your thoughts at any moment." I want to be mad at him for being too controlling but I can feel through our connection that he's doing it all to keep me safe. I can't get mad about that and I'm not ready to block him, anyways. Our mating isn't complete and until it is I want us open to each other.

"Alright Tennessee, you can come with me. I'd like to properly introduce you to my Daddy since you're gonna be around for awhile."

"Awhile?"

"Yes. What's wrong with awhile?"

"It's more like I'll be around till the good lord pulls the last breath from my body." He grabs me around my waist and pulls me to his chest. *"This is forever Bloom Michael, I'm not some teenage boy making promises I know I can't keep. I'm a shifter and when I promise you forever you better believe I mean it. Got it?"*

"Yes." It comes out more as a sigh. This man has succeeded in healing up the hole in my heart and now he's tattooing his name all over it, just in case someone has a question about who it belongs to.

Oh we're all his alright and he's all ours. My wolf grins from pointy ear to pointy ear.

"Good," he replies and then his mouth is on mine demanding I submit to his claim on me.

"What the heck just happened?" Bonnie asks breaking through the bubble that's just the two of us.

"What do you mean?" Emily asks looking back and forth between Bonnie and us.

"Instead of arguing they just stared at each other and then started to make out in front of us. Not that I'm complaining because that part was pretty ... wow! But still, what the heck?"

Laughing at Bonnie's description Emily explains, "They were talking through their mate connection. It looks like they resolved whether or not Pike is going with her and by the grin on his face I'd say he won."

"Wait, go back. What's this about a mate connection? Is that your way of saying they're psychic now?" Bonnie's brow scrunches up as she stares at us as if she just needs to look harder and she'll be able to see a string that connects us.

"No, it's not like that at all. They can't read everyone's minds, just each others. It's something special between mated pairs so they'll be able to protect and care for one another. It makes the mating easier especially when one of the mates isn't use to our ways. It's a lot easier to explain being connected when you have a way to prove it. Now that Pike is the alpha he'll be able to connect with all the pack members thoughts as well, though alpha's only use that ability when they sense someone could be hiding something dangerous to themselves or the pack."

"Please tell me that my moving into this wolf house of yours won't make me pack, because I'm so not ready for Big Bad here to be sorting through my most secret thoughts." She cocks her hip and stares at Pike waiting for an answer.

"No, Bonnie, you won't be official pack just by moving into the house. Though if you decide you want to become pack there is a way to do it. If you're gonna be living amongst us it might be something you'll want to consider."

Bonnie's face goes from one of relief to one of intrigue. She may not be ready to apply to be part of the pack today, but she isn't going to dismiss the idea either.

"I'll think about it, Big Bad."

"Okay, now that that was thrown out there, let's go get this stuff done. No offense to Ohio, but I'm ready to be home. So the sooner we get this done and get on the road the better." Emily's already headed to the door before anyone can respond and just before she steps outside she tosses over her shoulder, "Pike join me real quick. I need to have a word with ya."

Chapter 27 – Pike

~ I don't want to lose you ~

"You summoned me?" I know my voice drips of sarcasm, but as her alpha I don't appreciate being ordered around. Damn these women, not one of them are giving me the respect my position demands.

Emily waves her hand in my general direction; like she's trying to rid the air of my aggravation. "Pike, get over it. You may be my alpha and I respect that, but you're also my brother and I will always be your annoying little sister. So the best I can promise is when we're around the pack I'll keep my disrespect to a minimum, but any other time. Well, that'll depend on my mood."

I close my eyes and rub my temples. I just know a major headache is getting ready to pop up and being stuck in a car with these three for nine and half hours is not gonna help it.

"Emily Layke Masterson, did you drag me out here just to give me that speech?"

"Technically, I didn't drag you; you walked out on your own two feet."

"Emily!" Her name comes out as a growl.

She throws her hands to her hips. "Don't ya dare growl at me, Pike Lykos Masterson. See I know your full name too, and I'm not afraid to use it either."

I take a deep breath and release it then ask again through gritted teeth, "Okay sister dear, did you need something when you politely asked me to join you out here."

"Why yes, dear brother, I did."

"Emily, enough of this, just spit it out."

"Geez, you're no fun."

"Now!" I command.

"I was thinking about the Rose issue," She quiets her voice so only I'll be able to hear her.

"What about it? I told you I'm not bringing it up until we're safely back in Tennessee."

"I know, but the more I've thought about it, well … I think you need to tell her before we go. She needs to know what she's walking in to, Pike. Her mother is part of the pack she's joining. Hell, she has three half brothers she knows nothing about. As her mate you're suppose to protect her."

The wolf takes control and I grab Emily's arm, "I am protecting her. Don't ever accuse me of not doing so again."

She pushes me away, not even fazed by my outburst. "You're sending your mate into a situation you can't protect her from. She *will* be hurt by this, but if you warn her at least she won't be hurt by you keeping it from her, and she'll be able to prepare herself for what's getting ready to happen."

"I need her to go. If she finds out she might decide to stay here." There's vulnerability in my voice and I hate myself for letting it slip through.

"If you lie to her about it, she'll leave you anyway, and I doubt she'll come back. But, if you're up front with her you have a much better chance of keeping her. Tell her, Pike, you know it's the right thing to do."

"Fine, I'll do it after we visit her Daddy's grave." I sigh, my heart's heavy with the task I need to complete today that has nothing to do with packing. Heck, if this goes bad all the packing could've been for nothing.

Emily comes over and grabs me into a hug. "Good luck brother. I have faith she'll make the right choice."

"I just hope that choice doesn't take her away from me." I grip my sister tighter to my chest, I need the comfort of home, and my sister's the only piece of home I have with me.

The front door slams and the two girls from inside spill out onto the porch laughing. I know when they catch sight of Emily and me because the laughing abruptly stops.

"I'm sorry. I didn't … we didn't mean to interrupt. We just thought you'd be ready to leave," Bloom explains as she watches my face for any sign of what might have happened. I smile to reassure her everything's okay, but it doesn't reach my eyes, because I'm not sure it will be okay after we have our talk. She doesn't notice my apprehension, and I'm smart enough to keep our connection closed so she can't pick up on the thoughts running around my mind.

She walks down the stairs and grabs my hand, knotting her delicate slender fingers through my rough larger ones. I pull her hand to my mouth and kiss it gently which causes her to reward me with a soul warming smile.

Letting our hands fall back between us I ask, "Are you ready, darlin'?"

Squeezing my hand she replies, "Yep. Are you?"

"I am." Lord, I hope we are.***

She's still gripping my hand as we walk through the cemetery. We stopped and bought a bouquet of daisies to place on his grave and her other hand has those grasped against her chest.

The cemetery is located on the outside of town in the opposite direction of the cabin. There's a tiny white church at the front of the property that has a blood red door and the sides are covered in stained glass windows. A black wrought iron fence circles the whole property as do large maple trees. There are head stones scattered all around the grounds. I notice some newer stones, but most of the one's we pass are from the early 1900's.

At the back of the property, under one of the largest trees, Bloom pulls us to a stop and drops my hand. She takes a few more tentative steps then bends to place the bouquet on top of the headstone. I'm determined to stand back and give her the space she needs but when she crashes to her knees in front of the grave and begins to weep I rush to her side and pull her into my arms. She only stays there a few minutes before she pushes away from me and wipes her eyes.

"Thank you," she whispers as she smoothes her hand down my chest, not meeting my eyes.

I place my hand under her chin and make her look at me. "It'll always be my pleasure, darlin'."

Bloom nods then gently removes my hand from her face, placing it in hers on her lap. She turns back to her Daddy's tombstone.

"Daddy, I'm sorry I haven't visited before and I have no excuse good enough to explain why. I'm moving away and if you've been watching over me you probably already know what's been going on. I just wanted to say sorry for not coming sooner and I promise I'll come back to visit when we come back to town. Also, I wanted you to meet Pike. He's gonna take good care of me Daddy, and I don't want you up there worrying about me. I'll be okay."

She gets quiet and I send up a silent promise to Michael that I'll take care of his only daughter. We stay there on our knees, holding hands, for a long time. Bloom needs this, she needs me and I'm more than happy to give it to her. It might be the last thing she lets me do for her. When she stands up I join her and place my hand on her back, quietly showing my support. She leans down and traces her fingers over the inscription that reads: *Beloved Father and Husband.* When her fingers reach the husband part she jerks her hand back like the word burns her finger tips. I watch her face closely, she's deciding something and it's difficult for her to admit to herself what she'll have to do. Finally she kisses the tips of her fingers and places them back over the inscription and traces it all the way through letting her fingers linger over the last word.

"She didn't deserve you, Daddy, but I know you never stopped loving her. I don't think I'll ever be able to give her the kind of forgiveness you did, she doesn't deserve it, but I think I need her. She may be the only one who can give me the answers about who I really am." She closes her eyes and takes a deep breath before she finishes, "Bye Daddy, I'll always love you."

When she lets her hand drop back to her side I take the opportunity to guide her to a stone bench that sits closer to the church. She leans into me and I kiss the top of her head.

"I need to find her, Tennessee," she whispers. I love that she still uses her nickname for me and I sit there for a moment letting it soak in. There's a chance after I tell her she may not use it anymore. She'll probably come up with a harsher name to throw at me. I squeeze her tighter to my side for just a second more then I pull back so I can look down into her face.

"Bloom, I have something to tell you. I was planning to tell you even before you decided, I need you to know that, though I should've told you sooner." I watch her face crinkle in confusion and I push on when she doesn't say anything. "Rose, your mother, she's a member of our pack. I promise I didn't know when I first found you. Billy showed me her picture after he told me your parent's story. I was trying to find a way to tell you."

She pushes herself farther away from me. "How long?"

"I promise I've only known for a few days. I'm sorry I kept this from you."

"No, how long has my mother been with your pack?" She jumps to her feet and paces in front of the bench.

"I was around 4 or 5 when she joined our pack. Her mate had already been a member."

"She's been there ever since … ever since she left me."

"That's what it looks like. Bloom, talk to me baby, I promise I won't keep something like this from you again. Please, just tell me if you forgive me. I don't want to lose you," my voice cracks on the last sentence and I can feel my eyelids fighting to keep the tears inside.

Bloom stops pacing long enough to really look at me. I know I have to be a retched sight, my hands are shaking and I'm preparing to cry like a baby. She comes back and sits beside me and pulls my head into her neck and holds me. I can't hold the tears in any longer and they slide from my eyes soaking the shoulder of her shirt.

"I'm not mad at you, I'm mad at her. It had to be hard to tell me what you know and all that matters is that you told me. Do I wish she wasn't part of the pack? Yes. Will it stop me from coming with you? Hell, no. You're not losing me, Tennessee, and I'm not losing you over her. She's hurt me enough."

I pull back to look in her face, I can tell through our bond that she isn't lying, but I need to see her face to reassure myself. Her eyes glitter with the hurt her mother has caused, the understanding she's showing me and the unshed tears that threaten to spill down her cheeks. I place my hands on either side of her face and lean in to press my lips to hers. She willingly accepts my kisses, and when the tears finally fall from her eyes, she lets me wipe them away. When the last one has dropped she places one last kiss on my lips and pulls back.

I let my hands drop from her face so they can grab her hands. "Bloom, there's something else you need to know."

"Oh gosh, Pike, please tell me she isn't dead, because I'm not sure I can handle any more bad news," she says closing her eyes, like it'll keep out the bad news I'm getting ready to tell her.

"No, it's nothing like that, darlin'. Some might even consider it good news, but that's up for you to decide."

"Just tell me, fast, like it's a band aid you're pulling off. I can handle it come on." Her eyes are still closed and she's gripping my hands harder; hanging on for dear life, like this last revelation might be the one that breaks her.

"You have half brothers, three to be exact." Her eyes flick open as her mouth falls open, but nothing comes out, so I continue. "Tucker is the oldest, 19 he'll be 20 in a few months. He's my beta our second in charge. Then there's the twins Kyran & Killian, they just turned 18."

"I-I-I ... she has more children. I have brothers." I watch as she does the math in her head. "If Tucker is almost 20 that means ... she got pregnant right after she had me! Do they even know about me?"

"I'm certain they don't."

"AHHHHHH!" she screams slamming her fist down on the concrete bench. I grab it to make sure she hasn't done any damage, thankfully it isn't broken.

She stands jerking her hand from me and pointing her finger from the other hand at me. "That woman is a … well she's a bad word, and when we go to Tennessee I will be informing her of just the word she is and you will not stop me."

I stand up and pull her back into my chest so I can smooth my hand through the hair falling down her back. I have to suppress my chuckle. She's awfully cute when she's mad. "I would never try to."

"I may even slap her," she grumbles against my chest.

"I'm behind you no matter what you decide."

"What if I decide to punch her in the face?"

"I'll still be behind you, just promise me something," I say leaning back to push the hair back from her tear soaked face.

"What?"

"Use your other fist." I grab her swollen hand and continue, "I don't think this one can take much more damage, at least not for a few days."

Chapter 28 – Bloom

~ You should always go with your gut ~

Five hundred and eighty-two miles or roughly nine and half hours, that's how far it is from my old home in Ohio to my new home in Tennessee. That's how far I have to go till I'll be in the same town as my mother, the woman who abandoned me at birth to go start her new life with her new family. Am I angry? Hell yes I am, and sleeping on the news didn't help to squelch my anger at all, if anything it made it worse. Every time I closed my eyes last night I saw her raising her three boys, my brothers. She bandaged their scrapes, made them cookies, kissed them good night, and soothed them when they were crying. I bet they were raised to know about their wolf side, they weren't left to struggle with a part of them they never knew existed. Like me!

As mad as I am at Rose, I know I can't hold what she's done against my brothers. It's not their fault our mother is a ... well you know. Some also refer to a female dog by the same term.

Hey don't group me and that woman in the same category. I guess my wolf dislikes our "surrogate" as much as I do.

Anyways, those boys are the only family I have left (Rose doesn't count in my mind), and I want to get to know them. I hope they feel the same way when they find out about me.

"I can't speak for the twins, but I know Tucker and he'll want to know his only sister." Pike stretches his hand across the front seat of the sedan we're in to grab mine. I rub my thumb along the top of his hand and give him a little smile before I turn my eyes to stare at the scenery passing by us at 60 miles per hour.

"Tell me about them, please?" I plead.

"Pike, we've been on the road for hours. I've drank three bottles of water and if we don't find a ladies room real soon, you'll be cleaning a wet spot up back here before this rental is returned," Bonnie interrupts before Pike can tell me about them, I can't blame her though, it's not like she knows we're discussing them through our bond.

"Don't be so quick to soak your panties. There's a rest area a couple miles up ahead. Emily, text one of the guys and tell them to stop with us." The boys, Kit & Price, are two members of the pack that Pike had Tucker send to Ohio to drive our moving truck back to Tennessee. Pike doesn't want to be separated from us girls. He's still on high alert from Trace's attack on me. We haven't seen hide or hair of him since that night, and neither has anyone else in town, so Pike's convinced he's hiding out waiting for his next chance. I don't think he's brave enough to attempt anything else and I definitely don't think he'll follow us to Tennessee, not that he even knows that's where we're headed.

"I sent Kit the text. He said that's fine with them," Emily states from the back seat where she's sitting with Bonnie.

At the rest area each of the guys take turns watching over the girls' room, while the others do their business. They're sticking to the thought that we need to be guarded. After washing my hands I walk out to find myself alone in the lobby with Kit and Emily.

Kit Drake is easily six foot one and has auburn colored hair that is messy with curls that fall into his steel grey eyes. If Pike wasn't my own personal dream man come to life I could've easily fell for his crooked smile, just like Emily seems to be doing. The two are so close in height they can look directly into each other's eyes, which is exactly what they're doing. It's such an intimate moment, Emily's lips are parted in a soft smile that's so genuine and happy it tugs at my heart and Kit's is almost as bright though somehow I can tell he's trying to hold his back. He's the type of guy who will always hold his cards close to his heart until it's time for them to be revealed. The whole encounter has the butterflies in my gut working overtime and if Emily hadn't already explained to me that she isn't old enough to be mated, I would've guessed them to be mates.

"They might still be some day, darlin'. There is still time for that connection to hit them." Pike walks up behind me and wraps his arms around my middle, placing a kiss on my neck.

"I know, but seeing them together seems right. I feel it in my gut. Does that sound strange?" I turn in his arms to look up into his face. His eyes get distant as he contemplates my words then he looks back down at me and smiles.

"No, it doesn't sound strange. You should always go with what your gut is telling you, I've always followed mine and so far I love where it's led me. Right to you, darlin'." He leans in and presses a brief kiss to my

lips then releases me to address the group since Price and Bonnie have joined us.

"Alright, we're gonna get back on the road, but there's gonna be a little change. Price you're gonna ride in the back of our car with Bonnie. Emily you're gonna ride with Kit in the moving van." He looks at everyone to make sure there won't be any complaints and then claps his hands together and says, "Okay, let's hit the road. Bonnie try to refrain from drinking your weight in water because I'm not stopping again till we reach Tennessee. Once we're across the state border we'll stop and get lunch."

Emily looks at me and mouths "what the heck"? I shrug my shoulders though I know her brother's trying to give her and Kit more time alone. I'm slowly learning that my mate's worse than one of the old busy bodies that come around Billy's trying to fix me up with some long lost nephew. A complete and utter meddler, I make one comment and he's ready to plan the wedding.

"I hear spring's a good time to get married." Pike laughs in my head.

"Ha ha, weren't you the one who just told me they had time?" I ask climbing back into the passenger seat of the car.

"I wasn't talking about them, darlin'."

"Then who are you talking ...." I looked over at him after fastening my seat belt and he winks at me.

"Oh no, Tennessee, we have more than enough hurdles to cross right now without throwing a wedding into the mix. Plus if you're gonna propose to me it better not be in the front seat of a rental car that smells like sweaty feet." Crap, that came out kind of mean, I hope he isn't serious.

He stares at me for several long moments then starts laughing so hard he doubles over against the steering wheel. Once he's able to contain himself he leans in and grabs my neck pulling me to the center of the car so his lips can meet mine. He pulls back from the kiss to press his forehead against mine and whispers, "God, I love you."

OH MY GOSH!

He loves me, but it's only been a week. I lean back so I can look into his eyes. "Already?"

You're his mate. Stop questioning if he loves us, of course he does. Geesh! My wolf shakes her head at me though I can tell she's glowing from his declaration just as much as me.

He skims his fingers along my cheek down to my lips. "Since the first moment I saw you walking through those woods determined to help an injured animal."

We're moving so fast, it's only been a week since he came barreling into my life and half of that week he spent in his wolf form pretending to be a dog, but my heart's screaming for me to say those words back to him. He's surrendered his heart to me and I feel the need to surrender mine to him.

I grab the hand he has touching my face and kiss his palm, then lean in to kiss his lips. "I love you too, Tennessee."

"The two of you are so sweet; you're liable to give me a toothache. Can we please get on the road now?" Bonnie jokes from the back seat. I turn to find Price looking at her like she grew a second head and I have to laugh when Bonnie notices to and asks, "What? You're thinking it too, it's not my fault you're afraid to say it because he's the big bad alpha."

Dang, my friend's leaning heavily on her sass this week. I hope she remembers her sweet side is just as good.

"She'll be ok, darlin'. She's only using it to protect herself."

"What does she need to protect herself from?"

"Bloom, you're not the only one who's faced a lot of revelations this week. Bonnie also found out there are shifters and that her closest friend is one. Not to mention she saw you attacked. So give her some time to adjust to her new world. She'll go back to herself once she does."

"Goodness, I hadn't even thought of that. No wonder she's been acting this way."

"She'll be fine. Don't worry darlin'."

"I'll hold you to that, Tennessee."

"Oh, I love when you hold me." I roll my eyes at him as I pull out of our connection.

Price is looking between Bonnie and Pike; I can tell he's waiting to see if my mate will do anything about her outburst. I'm quickly learning pack members are not suppose to disrespect the alphas, but Price hasn't learned yet that Bonnie isn't pack and even if she were she would always speak her mind. It's one of the things I love about the girl and there's no way I'm gonna ask her to change just to appease some uptight wolves.

"Calm down, wolf, Bonnie means no harm. She's all bark and no bite," Pike reassures the younger man.

"Hey now, you don't know I might bite." She turns to Price and winks with a huge grin across her plump face. "At the very least I nibble."

Price flushes ten shades of red before his skin finally turns back to its normal creamy white. He really is a handsome guy. He's only an inch taller than me, but he makes up for his lack of height by being pure muscle. Price looks like a fighter, or with his dark brown hair buzzed that way, maybe I should say a soldier. Yes, I can easily see him with dog tags hanging around his neck, but no he's a wolf. That means there will be no life in the military for this brown eyed man. He's sworn his life to his fellow pack members and he'll die before he breaks that promise.

"You've become rather intuitive, darlin'." Pike says through our connection.

"Hmm, how do you mean?" I ask turning my attention to him.

"What you were thinking about Price. About a year ago he thought about joining the army instead of staying with our pack, but his loyalty to us won out. I'm thankful for that, I know he'll be a valuable member, but you just met him. How can you know all this?" The question is asked more to himself than to me.

"Just like how I felt about Emily and Kit. I feel it in my gut."

"Have you always been able to sense things about people or is this a new discovery?"

I think about the question for a few minutes as I play my past through my mind as if it's on fast forward. There are numerous times in my life I've had the same gut instinct about someone or a situation, so no this isn't new.

"I've always had this knack of reading people. It's how I knew Bonnie would be my best friend and how I knew that Trace was no good. But the last one came a little too late for me to steer clear." I pause then ask, *"Is this another shifter thing?"*

"No, darlin', it's not. I believe I should follow my gut, but it seems yours can do a lot more than mine. We should probably bring this up to the elders also when we meet with them."

"If you think it could mean something."

"It might, but don't worry love we'll figure this out together." He reaches across the seat and rubs my knee to reassure me, but I'm to wound with this new discovery to let his touch comfort me the way it should.

Once we cross the Tennessee line we stop at a diner to have lunch. Pike and I finish before everyone else so we decide to wait on them outside. He leans against the car and I curl up to him with my back to his front and his arms wrapped around me. There's a rain storm getting ready to come through and the wind is starting to pick up speed. I watch as a flyer is picked up and tossed around the parking lot then swept away. I hear the bell on the diner's door ring and it pulls my attention from the flyer just as the others step out of the small building with Emily and Kit bringing up the rear. The gust causes Emily's hair to fly back from her face and in that instant I see Kit take in a deep breath and I know.

"Tennessee, they're mates," I whisper so only he can hear me.

"We discussed this, darlin', they could be but they're still too young." He's watching the cars passing by, probably keeping an eye out for Trace, instead of looking at the event taking place at the front of the diner.

My eyes are still locked on Kit and Emily. He's leaning into her neck taking a deeper whiff with her none the wiser. I can barely contain the giddiness in my voice when I say, "No, not might be, they are. Look!" I grip his chin turning his face in the right direction.

Kit turns Emily gently by the shoulders so she's facing him. Her face is one of complete surprise and joy when he leans in and brushes his lips to hers.

When she threads her fingers through his hair to deepen the kiss, I turn away to give them the privacy they deserve.

"H-how is this? It's too soon, I need to stop this." Pike moves to go over to them, but I grab his arm to catch his attention.

"No Tennessee, it's their time. Don't ruin it for them by acting like the over protective big brother." I place my palm to his cheek because I know my touch calms him.

"But …" He starts to grumble.

"No buts. We were just talking about how they looked like mates and you we're forcing them to spend time alone together, so you are not getting upset because their mating happened sooner than you wanted." I pull away from his arms and I'm facing him with my hands on my hips.

"You're right, darlin', sorry it's just hard to see this happen to my little sister so soon. I thought I'd have a few more years before I'd lose her to her mate."

"Pike, you're not losing Emily. She'll always be your sister, just now she's gonna be your mated sister and there'll be a new family member." I turn to look at Kit and Emily again. His hands are on her face looking deep into her eyes as if he stares long enough he'll learn all her secrets. Emily's hands are fisted into the sides of his t-shirt holding his body as close to hers as possible. They exude happiness so I say, "Tennessee, look at them. He's going to take over being her protector. He'll love her and provide for her. They're going to balance each other the way they were made too. They've both waited for this since they were kids and now they get it."

He looks at his sister and Kit then he looks back at me searching my face for something though I'm not sure what. When he pulls me back to his chest he asks,

"How do you know all of this? Until the other day you didn't even know about the mate bond."

Looking up into his ocean colored eyes I begin, "I just feel it in my …"

"In your gut, I know," he cuts me off with a chuckle.

"Alright, will someone tell me why we have a love fest going on instead of being back on the road? First you guys get all mushy in the car, now Emily and Kit have joined the sickeningly sweet couple club. Have you two seen how they're staring at each other?" Bonnie asks pointing at the new mates who've finally realized they have an audience and break apart to walk over and join us, holding hands, of course.

"Alpha …" Kit begins.

Pike holds up his hand to stop his words, pulls the other man into a hug and says, "Congratulations.

We'll announce yours and Emily's bond when we get back to the pack."

"Thank you, but how did you know?" Kit pulls back from the hug.

"It seems my Bloom can tell things about people. She had a feeling earlier you two would be mates and she saw when it happened." Pike turns to his sister and grabs her into an even bigger hug than he gave Kit.

When he's done I took my turn congratulating the new couple. As I release Emily she looks at Pike asking, "How can she? I've never heard of anything like that happening."

"I think your brother is exaggerating. I just had a gut feeling you two were mates, he makes it sound way more mystical than it was." I try to brush it off. I don't want to deal with anymore than what is already on my plate.

"Your gut has been right on twice today, darlin'," Pike says arching one eye brow in challenge.

"Twice?" Price asks joining the conversation after him and Bonnie also congratulate Emily and Kit.

"She was assessing your character in her thoughts and could tell you were a soldier at heart," Pike explains.

"Very few people know I was considering that," Price admits as he reassesses what he thinks of me.

"Ya'll are wolf shifters. You've had to have seen some way crazy things in your lives that us normal humans probably don't even know exists, so why are you staring at Blu like she's something rare? No offense, Blu," Bonnie asks when the other members of our group begin staring at me.

"None taken, Bon."

"We're not use to someone's *gut* being so in tune. It's not a normal thing among shifters," Pike tries to explain.

"Okay, well I have to say this mating bond thingy seems to be rubbing off on everyone in this vicinity," she waves her hands in big circles in our direction then turns to Price and narrows her eyes at him. "You keep your distance. I am not looking to be tied to one furry overprotective wolf, ever!"

"Umm, you do realize the mating bond isn't some cold you can catch, right?" Price asks her back.

"Either way, soldier boy, I'm not taking my chances. Keep your distance." She turns her attention to me, "And Bloom if you even get a tingle in your gut about me being mated to anyone, take some pepto and get rid of that tingle fast."

"I can't take pepto to get rid of a gut feeling, Bon."

"Have you ever tried?" She asks with her hand on her hip as she watches me seriously.

"Well, no," I admit.

"Then you can't say it won't work. Pepto helps with a lot of stomach issues, gut instincts might be another to add to the list."

Chapter 29 – Pike

~ 20 years in the making ~

Before we even pass into the Paxton borders I feel the pack members. They're excited for their alpha to be home and I'm just as excited to be back with my mate in toe. Very few have been privilege to that little bit of information, though soon the whole pack will know I found her. I had Tucker call a pack meeting for tonight, but before I can announce it to everyone I have to tackle the biggest obstacle of letting my mate meet her brothers and confront her mother.

When I talked to Tucker about the pack meeting I told him to make sure the house is clear when we get home. I don't want anyone asking questions about our newest house mates until I'm ready to answer those questions. So when we pull up to the house I'm not surprised to find the garage empty of all but a handful of cars.

I give the girls very little time to take in their new surroundings before I rush them to their new accommodations. I promise to give them both a tour of the place after the meeting is over, and they don't seem to mind the delay. I've explained to both of them what the priorities of their first day here will be and they didn't grumble too much.

"Are you guys like the Bill Gates of the shifter world? Only someone with that kind of green could afford a place like this," Bonnie's standing in the middle of her suite taking in the room in a slow circle.

"Let's just say we've made some good investments. Every member of the pack gets an equal share of the pack holdings so no-one here wants for anything no matter what their rank may be."

"What kind of investments?" She can be worse than a two year old who's just learned the word why and I normally don't mind but our day is packed and I don't have time to break out the pack portfolio to satisfy her curiosity.

"Bonnie, I promise I'll explain more to you about everything here, but right now I'd like to show my mate to our suite before she has to meet with Rose and her brothers." I have my arm around Bloom when I explain this and I don't miss her whole body flinching at her mother's name. It's eating at me that I can't save her from the hurt this meeting is going to cause her.

"Oh Blu, I'm sorry. Are you sure you don't want me to come with you?" Bonnie comes back to us and takes both of Blooms hands into her own. As hard as this girl comes across it warms my heart knowing that when it comes to Bloom she shows her nothing but love and loyalty. Bonnie would make a wonderful pack member and I intend to formally extend an invitation for her to join, as soon as we get today's business handled and all the drama I know is coming settled down.

"Thanks for the offer, Bon, but I need to try to do this alone." Bloom smiles at her friend trying to reassure her even though I can feel through the bond that she isn't as confident as she's letting on.

"Not completely alone, I hope," Bonnie says turning her gaze to glare at me.

"I don't plan on leaving her side. No worries," I promise.

"Still, if you need any back up just text me and I'll be there in heartbeat, well as long as I don't get lost in this place. Which there's a good chance of that happening if I venture far from this room, so just take notes on who I need to smack down and I'll get them later."

"I'll make sure Tennessee plays secretary and keeps a meticulous list of everyone that needs beat down. Try not to get lost. I don't want to have to send out the wolf search party to find ya."

"I can't guarantee anything, but I'll try to be good and if I go anywhere I'll leave a trail of bread crumbs like Hansel & Gretel."

"Maybe leave a trail of non-edible items. It'll be safer, because these shifters eat more like pigs than wolves and I don't want them eating your way back to your room."

"Thanks for the heads up, my friend. Now get your behind on the move I need to get settled in and so do you." She pulls Bloom into her arms and whispers, "Good luck. Remember no matter how it goes I love you and have your back."

"I know, Bon. I love you too," Bloom whispers back then releases the hug, "Come on Tennessee, time for you to show me our room."***

"What do you think of your new home, darlin'?" She walked around the suite taking it all in when we'd first got there, but that's been 20 minutes ago and she's yet to say a word whether she likes it or not.

"It's beautiful, Tennessee." She puts her hand out for me to take and I do so willingly. "There's a lot I'm gonna have to take in today and I'd be lying if I said I'm not nervous. So I'm sorry if I'm not responding the way you hoped. I really do love this suite."

I caress her face with my free hand. "It's fine, darlin'. I know how nervous you are, but please remember I'll be by your side all day. You'll probably get sick of my presence and try to send me away."

"When are they supposed to be here?"

"About an hour, would you like to take a bath before they arrive? It might help you relax."

"That sounds like a good idea. I'm feeling rather icky from being in the car all day." She leans in and kisses my cheek then heads towards the bathroom.

"I'll let you know when they get here." She stops at the door that leads to our bath and asks, "Will you have Rose come first. I want to talk with her alone before I meet my brothers."

"Of course, darlin'."

Forty-five minutes later she's done with her bath and leaning against me on the couch. The knock on the door has her sitting straight up with her feet planted flat on the floor. I want to pull her back to my side because my body feels the loss of hers but I know now isn't the time, so I run my hand down her bare arm to soothe her then get up to answer the door.

Rose is standing there with her mate Grady. I shouldn't be surprised to see him by her side but since I sent out a cryptic request to meet with her before the pack meeting, it rubs my wolf wrong that he ignored the part of the message that said to come alone. I stomp down the urge to make him get to his knees and beg for forgiveness for ignoring my orders, this is going to be hard enough without me throwing my dominance on the older man, so I plaster a fake smile on my face and usher them into the living room.

I expect the shit to hit the fan as soon as they take in the sight of Bloom sitting on the couch, but Bloom isn't even in the room. Trying to be gracious I say, "Have a seat, please. I'll be right back."

"Darlin', where are you?"

"The kitchen, sorry my throat was dry so I came to get a glass of water. Also, I need a minute to collect myself, Tennessee. Maybe you can explain what this meeting is about without including the part that the daughter she abandoned is here and your mate."

"Okay, sugar. Do you mind bringing out some drinks for us and our guests? You might not try to slap her right away if you have something in your hands when you join us."

"Very funny, I don't think I'll attack her as soon as I see her. Though depending on her attitude it might happen, but I'll bring the darn drinks."

"And Bloom."

"Yes Tennessee?"

"Don't put poison in Rose's drink."

"Darn, I guess I better dump this glass down the drain. See ya in a few minutes."

"Good idea. Love you, darlin'."

"I love you too, Tennessee." It warms my heart how freely she's saying those words back to me since we

uttered them that morning in the car, but right now I have other things to focus on so I pull out of our connection and sit down on the other couch that faces our guests.

"Alpha, why have you asked me here?" Rose is sitting next to her husband with her legs crossed and she's fidgeting with the hem of her navy skirt. She looks so much like Bloom that it breaks my heart for my mate all over again. The only differences are that Rose's hair is cut short in an A-line bob that falls just below her chin and her eyes are the color of emeralds. Rose looks older but not by much. Her skin is relatively wrinkle-free other than a few laugh lines around her eyes and mouth.

"I found my mate while I was away," I announce the fake smile still plastered to my face.

"Oh, Ike congratulations," she uses the shortened version of my name the way my mother use to do. The fist that has been gripping my heart since my parents' deaths squeezes a little tighter. I take a deep breath to center my thoughts and then I continue.

"Thanks, but that's not the only reason you're here. She …" Bloom chooses that moment to walk in the room. She carries the tray holding a pitcher of lemonade and glasses of ice to the coffee table that sets between the two couches then sits beside me. Hers and Rose's eyes are locked on each other as we all wait to see who will speak first.

"Bloom?" Rose asks as if the carbon copy of herself sitting directly across from her could be anyone other than her only daughter.

Bloom has apparently slipped on a mask of indifference because when she answers Rose though you can't see any emotion in her response. "Yes, I'm your daughter."

Rose looks frantically between Bloom and I then turning to her mate and whispers, "I don't know what's going on."

He put his arm around her then looks at me, "Alpha Pike, what's the point of this? You can see how much this is hurting my mate."

I jump to my feet and spit out my words between growls, "And you don't think this hurts my mate?" I want to lunge at the older wolf and rip him apart for thinking his mate hurting these few moments is anywhere near the pain my mate has been put through since birth.

Bloom breaks through my angry haze by taking my hand and pulling me back to her side on the couch.

"Pike baby, calm down. He doesn't mean any harm. I don't think they even put together I'm your mate until your outburst." She lets her mask slip long enough while she speaks so I can see all the love she has to

offer me. When she places her lips to mine I feel the last of the anger leave my body.

I turn back to our guests. Both of their faces show how shocked they are and tears are filling Rose's eyes. "We didn't arrange this meeting to hurt you." Not that I care if her feelings are hurt. "It's just that Bloom is my mate and has agreed to move here to be with me. No thanks to you," I glare at Rose and she at least has the good nature to look ashamed of herself, "she is finally learning what she is."

"You left me with no answers. What if I had shifted?" Bloom's anger is finally breaking through her carefully crafted mask. She's now sitting on the edge of her seat with her eyes focused on Rose.

"Billy would've called me."

"You shouldn't have put *your* responsibility off on someone who knows very little about our kind!" My mate's voice rises with each word she speaks.

"I was going to take you, but Billy wouldn't let me," Rose finally says trying to defend herself.

"No, you don't get to use that excuse. You could have at least visited me, let me get to know you. Get to know my brothers! But you decided it would be easier on you and your new life if you just left me without any knowledge of who I really am!" She's standing now and I'm keeping a hold of one of her hands to keep her from leaping across the coffee table to get into her mother's face.

Grady stands to step in front of his mate. "Now calm down, you don't know what she's been through."

It was the worst thing he could've done. Bloom pushes the tray of drinks off the coffee table and hops up onto it so she can be eye to eye with the six foot seven wolf. She jams her fisted hands onto her hips and stares the man down. It's the sexiest, most reckless thing I think I've seen her do yet.

She keeps connected with his glare as she narrows her eyes. Her next words come out closer to a growl, "You *will not* protect her from this. It has been 20 years in the making. So your best bet is to back down now before I rip out your throat for getting in my way. I didn't come here to hurt either of you but if I'm not allowed to speak my peace I won't hesitate in taking out my anger in more violent forms on both of you. Sit. Down. Now!"

There is no way around it, my mate means what she says and I don't doubt my spitfire will follow through. Thankfully Grady has the good sense to sit back down and shut up. I'll say he even looks a little frightened of his step-daughter.

She turns back to her mother. "You owe me a lot of answers and you will give them all to me. We will be spending time together and do not mistake it for me forgiving you at all. You are a means to an end for me and that is it. I will not call you mother, mom, mama or any other form of that word. I will be living in this town and I know we will be forced to interact at pack events but unless I approach you first you will not attempt to speak with me. Do you understand so far?"

Rose nods. Tears are streaming down her cheeks now and she's visibly shaking. Bloom however is completely still as she's able to release the anger she's pent up the last 20 years.

"Last, I plan on getting to know my brothers. They are the only family I have left, since my Dad died, and you will be staying here to face their questions about me. You will not lie about abandoning me to make yourself look better."

At this news Rose looks up at Bloom, "M-Michael died? H-how did it happen?"

At the mention of her Dad I watch Bloom soften up a little, "Yes, a year ago. He fell asleep behind the wheel coming home from work."

Rose's left hand flies to her mouth while her right hand reaches for her daughter, "Oh Bloom, I'm so sorry."

Bloom pulls back. "Thank you, but no. You don't get to comfort me through this. You lost that privilege when you left me alone in a hospital at birth."

Rose pulls her hand back to her stomach as if Bloom's words have punched her in the gut. Bloom ignores her mother's reaction as she steps down from the coffee table and looks at me, "I'm sorry I made a mess, Tennessee. If you'll show me where the cleaning supplies and towels are I'll clean it up before the others get here."

"This is your home too, darlin', so you can mess it up as often as you want." I caress her cheek then say, "I'll go get the supplies. Have a seat."

Chapter 30 – Bloom

~ Looks like we'll really be family now ~

Pike goes and gets the supplies to clean up my mess. This has gotten out of hand fast, but I can't regret it. She needs to know how badly she hurt me. I could've probably let her know a little calmer, but once I got started I couldn't calm down. Even now I'm still seeing red.

Pike walks back into the room, a bucket of water and towels in his hand. I reach for the supplies but he won't hand them over, so I bend down and pick up the pitcher and glasses. Thankfully, they hit the rug instead of the hardwood floors so they didn't shatter. Pike uses one towel to soak up the lemonade and the other he dips into the water to wipe down the spot down. The whole time we are doing this Rose sits sobbing and Grady sits beside her not moving. I try to worry about the mess in front of me and ignore them, but once the mess is gone and I'm forced to sit back on the couch in front of them, I can no longer hold my tongue.

"Good lord, Grady, comfort your mate so she'll stop the crying. The boys should be here anytime and she needs to calm down so she'll be able to answer any questions they have." My words sink into the older man because he finally takes in the condition of his mate; pulling her into his arms he whispers words of comfort to her.

Pike comes back into the room from disposing of the cleaning supplies and sits down beside me. He takes my hand into his and we sit in silence. At that moment I have no more to say to the couple across from us and apparently neither does Pike.

After several more minutes Rose stops crying and reaches for a tissue and compact out of her purse to clean up her face. She closes the compact then tosses it and the tissue back into her purse and turns to me.

"Bloom, I wish I had handled it all differently. I never meant to push my daughter so far away."

"That may be the case, but you can't go back and change it now," I sigh then continue, "I don't want to hate you Rose. My Dad wouldn't be happy with me if I did, but I'm not ready to forgive you. I may never be able too. I do need you though, because like I said you may be the only one who can answer the questions about who I am."

"Pike has already told you that you're a shifter, so I'm not sure what else I can help you to understand."

"I never shifted and from what he's told me it's very odd and now there's this … gut thing."

"Gut thing?" She looks truly confused.

"It seems that I can …" There's a knock on the door before I can finish. Pike moves to answer it and I listen as he greets the three boys.

"So, where is the girl who's stolen our alpha's heart?" The voice that asks is warm and friendly. I stand up from the couch and look towards the hall they're coming from. Pike enters first and crosses to stand beside me. The other three stop right inside the door side by side and stare at me.

"This is my mate, Bloom Daniels." Pike puts his arm around my waist and gives me a squeeze. The boys say nothing; just continue to stare at me. I know they catch my resemblance to Rose, it's pretty hard to miss if you've ever seen her. All three of them look me over from head to toe then turn their attention to their mother. Their eyes are a mixture of confusion and I know one of them is seconds from demanding an explanation.

Finally Rose speaks up, "Boys stop being rude and come greet your sister."

Two of them shout "Sister!" and the other turns his eyes back to glare at me. Rose proceeds to explain about her marriage to my father ending with how she abandoned me at birth. Pike picks up the story to tell them how we found each other and how until the other day I didn't know shifters even existed. When they finish talking the tallest one on the end crosses to me pulling me into a hug.

"Damn, I have a sister." He pulls back to look down at me and says, "Bloom, I'm Tucker. Most people around here call me Tuck." Tucker looks a lot like his father; they have the same light brown hair except Tuckers is to his shoulders in loose layers and the same bright amber eyes. Tucker is taller than Grady by a couple inches, putting him close to seven feet. Having just been hugged by him I can tell he's pure muscle. I understand why he's Pike's beta, my brother is deadly if he needs to be, though my gut is telling me he's extremely laid back and completely loyal to my mate.

"I'm so happy to meet you Tuck. Most people call me Bloom, but my friends call me Blu. Feel free to call me either." I have to step back to smile at him. He returns my smile then turns to Pike, "Looks like we'll really be family now."

Pike grins at him and says, "Yes, brother, we will be." They give each other a one armed hug that guys normally give that includes a pound on the back, and then Tucker moves to take a seat on the couch beside us.

The twins watch the whole exchange without saying a word. Though they are twins the only thing they have in common is their height, unlike Tucker who is a mountain of a man, they aren't much taller than me and are a lot leaner than their older brother. The one that is glaring at me has Rose's hair color and Grady's eyes but his features are far more angular and harsh than either of his parents. His blonde hair is cut short on the sides but longer on the top so it can be spiked. The other twin is the spitting image of his

Dad, in a shorter package, but he has Rose's bright emerald eyes. His light brown hair is cut shorter in the back and he has long bangs in the front that keep falling over his left eye. He gives me a shy smile then comes to hug me like Tucker did.

Releasing me he introduces himself, "I'm Killian and this is my twin Kyran. We're both pleased to meet you." My gut tells me Killian is being sincere, but Kyran doesn't feel the same. It also tells me that Killian and his inner wolf are gentle souls, who very rarely give into the darker part of their nature. Kyran on the other hand is anger and darkness wrapped up like a tight ball that's getting ready to unravel. It scares me seeing that in my own brother, but if my gut is right then I know it's the truth.

"I'm pleased to meet you too, Killian." He nods then steps away to sit beside his mother. I breathe a sigh of relief when Kyran doesn't move to hug me but instead sits in one of the chairs at the end of the coffee table.

Pike sits me down between him and Tucker on the couch then addresses the room, "Now that that is done I need to let you know there is a chance Bloom is in danger." He relays what happened with Trace and how he has yet to be located. Apparently there are still some of his wolves back in Ohio looking for him with no success.

"I want everyone on alert watching for any outsiders who come to town. He may not have followed us, but I don't want to take any chances with Bloom's or Bonnie's safety. I plan on announcing all of this at tonight's pack meeting as well, but seeing as you're her family as well I wanted to tell you first."

"Who's Bonnie?" Tucker leans forward with his elbows resting on his knees and looks at Pike.

"She's Bloom's best friend who moved here with us. She's going to live with the pack for a while, possibly permanently," Pike explains. "We gave her a suite in the single's section of the house. She's there now getting unpacked."

"What do you mean the singles section?" I ask Pike through our connection.

"The house suites are broken out into sections: mated pairs, single pack members, the elders, and then the top ranking members. None of the sections are any better than another, and everyone is free to decorate their suite as they please. It's just easier to keep the singles, who tend to have loud parties, away from mated pairs because they usually have little ones and don't want them woken up by the loud noises."

"That makes sense."

Kyran, who has been glaring at me the whole time Pike explained what's going on, jumps up and growls, "It's bad enough that you brought her here, but now you are risking our lives by letting a human outsider to live among us, all because she can't be here without her friend."

At once all of the men jump up to hold back Pike, who has moved to attack Kyran. Tucker is holding Pike's arms back, snarls at his younger brother, "Get out of here now you little fool, before your Alpha decides he'd like to use your fur as a rug."

Kyran narrows his eyes at me, "My mother should have killed you in the womb to save us all the trouble I know you're going to cause this pack." Pike breaks free of the three grown men who are holding him back, but Kyran had already bolted from the room after the last word was uttered.

I know Pike is going to follow Kyran and kill him for what he's said to me, but I can't let that happen. Moving in front of him I place my hands on the sides of his face, "Tennessee, please calm down, I don't need to lose anymore family."

"He threatened you and I will make him pay for it," Pike's wolf is in charge and staring at the hall that leads out of the suite, he wants to chase down the threat.

"Then punish him somehow, but please don't kill my brother," I plead with the wolf.

Oh come on, let him take that little weasel out. My wolf pipes in.

Pike finally looks at me and places his hands over top of mine on his face, "Mate, please tell me why I shouldn't kill him? I saw what your gut was telling you about him, evil and darkness. He is dangerous to all of us."

"We don't know if my gut is right and he said what he did because he's hurt. This was all a lot to take in and apparently he couldn't handle that, but that's no reason for him to die."

Stop fooling yourself. Our gut is never wrong. That brother of ours is trouble with a capital T and should be taken out now before he wrecks everything. My wolf snaps at me as she paces back in forth through my subconscious.

I can tell Pike is back in charge of himself when he quirks his eyebrows at me down playing my gut feelings.

"Okay, my gut is probably right, but that doesn't mean he can't redeem himself."

"Wait, I'm sorry to interrupt, but what is this about gut feelings?" Tucker asks. I hadn't realized but he is the only one who remains in the room with us. The others must have gone after Kyran.

Pike sighs then says, "Sit down, Tuck. There is more you need to know about your sister." He tells him how I knew about Emily and Kit and about the way

I've been reading people. Tucker takes it all in and then when Pike is done asks, "So you can't shift?"

"No, but ever since Pike has revealed himself I've been able to feel my wolf. She's there in the back of my thoughts; she just can't come out like yours."

"Wow, I'm sorry sis. I can't imagine having my wolf locked away." It makes me smile at how easy he has slipped into the role of brother.

"It's hard now that I know she's there and I'm determined to find out what's causing her to be locked away."

"I'll help anyway I can. It might have something to do with your *gut* instincts though. Do you know if there's a history of *gut* instincts on your Dad's side?"

"My Dad never said anything and I have no other living family members on his side to ask."

Tucker comes over and pulls me into another hug, "Ah sis, don't worry you have family now and we'll figure this all out together."

"Okay, Tuck, now that you're caught up I want you to go keep an eye on Kyran. We have the pack meeting soon and I don't want him coming to cause trouble." Pike is pacing the room, trying to calm himself down. I know he's still aching to kill my brother, but because I've asked he isn't going too.

"I'm on it, brother. Operation keep the moronic possibly evil brother away from pack meeting is a go." He winks at me and I know he's trying to be funny to calm Pike down, and thankfully it works because Pike and I are both still laughing as Tucker walks out of the suite.

Chapter 31 – Pike

~ She'll make one hell of an addition ~

I pull Bloom into the side of my body so I can wrap my arm around her waist. I have just introduced her and Bonnie to the pack, and though they seem to take the news of my mate being Rose's daughter pretty well, I know she'll be the hot topic in the pack tomorrow.

"You know we could've left out the part about Rose being my mom," Bloom grumbles through our connection though outward she's still smiling at the pack as they all come up to greet her.

"Darlin', you can't deny someone when she's your spitting image."

"We could force her to have plastic surgery. Turn her into the pack's version of Joan Rivers."

"Too late for that darlin', the pack has already seen you and they've known Rose long enough to know what she looks like."

"Dang, well keep it in mind for later. I might get tired of hearing people talk about how much we look alike."

"Ok, darlin'." I give her side a reassuring squeeze as she shakes yet another hand and then say, *"Heads up, the elders and their mates are coming over."*

Her head swings around searching the room, she easily finds the group that's descending upon us and plasters on her warmest smile, *"We need them to help, Tennessee."*

"Don't worry, darlin', they'll love you so much they'll be begging to help."

"Pike, I'm so pleased to hear our Kit and your Emily are mates. They make such a wonderful pair." Isla

Drake greets me wrapping me up in her arms the same way she's been doing since I was a little boy. Isla is 46 and has long curly hair the same auburn color as her son, Kit. She is petite for a wolf only reaching five foot five to her mate Noah's six foot one. She's the peace keeper on the council and I know she'll love Bloom, not just because I do, it'll be because Isla loves everyone she meets. My mom use to say Isla could find the good in a serial killer.

"I'm awful pleased, too. Emily's pretty darn lucky to be getting you as a mother-in-law. I might have to tag along to some of your family dinners with her so I can steal me some of your down home cookin'."

She pats my chest and laughs, "You are always welcome at my table. But there is no need to wait, anytime you want some of my food you just call me up and I'll whip some up for ya." Isla turns her smile to Bloom and says, "Now, introduce me to this beautiful girl of yours."

I place my hand on the small of Blooms back, "Darlin', this is Elder Isla Drake and her mate Noah. Isla, Noah, this is my mate Bloom Daniels." Bloom stretches out her hand expecting the elder to shake it, but Isla being Isla pulls my mate into the same kind of hug she's just given to me.

Isla releases Bloom from the hug, "Welcome to our pack Bloom. I look forward to getting to know you as our new Alpha female and hopefully as a new friend."

"That is very sweet of you, thank you Elder Isla." Bloom gives the older woman a genuine smile. "Please, say you'll come to our suite tomorrow morning for breakfast. We're inviting all the Elders to discuss some issues and I'd love it if you'd join us."

Isla returns the smile and nods, "I wouldn't miss it for the world." Then turning to her mate and grabbing his arm, "Come on, Noah, we don't want the rest of the wolves to get mad because we're monopolizing the new mates." Noah nods at me and shakes Bloom's hand then follows after his mate. He isn't being rude. Noah is just a quiet man who is content to let Isla do the talking for both of them. Though I know never to confuse his being quiet as him being weak, I have seen Noah (in his wolf form) take down a 12 point buck like it was nothing more than wobbly legged fawn.

Isla and Noah are followed by Price's parents Fina and Lucas Greene. Elder Fina is a pistol who lives up to her fire engine red hair. I'm certain if you look up the definition of sassy in the dictionary you'll find a picture of Fina beside it. She grabs me into a hug then proceeds to ignore me to give my mate attention.

"Now, I don't know what happened between you and that momma of yours, but I know a rift when I see one, and I'm here to tell you that if you need help putting your momma in her place for whatever she screwed up you holler at ole Fina. You hear me?" Fina informs Bloom of this as she's holding her in a tight hug, not much different than the one Isla had just given her.

"Um …" Bloom looks at me and then back at Fina before she finishes with a, "yes ma'am."

"Good, now we'll see you kids in the morning for this breakfast you're hosting. Do you need me to bring anything? Pastries, fruit, liquor?"

"Liquor for breakfast?" Bloom asks as Lucas Greene steps around his wife to give her a hug.

"Doll, with that many dominate wolves in one room, you're gonna need something to cut through the testosterone."

"Um …"

"Fi don't scare the girl before she gets a chance to know us," Lucas chastises his wife then turns back to Bloom and says, "Don't listen to this one. Us males aren't that bad, fill our stomachs with some good home cookin' and we'll be so sated that we won't even think of attacking each other. At least for a good forty minutes."

Blooms mouth drops open and Lucas chuckles. I lean into her and whisper, "Darlin', he's pulling your leg." She looks at me then Lucas and he gives her a wink accompanied by a wolfish grin then saunters away with his wife, still chuckling.

Elder Cathal Burke and his mate Shea walk up and introduce themselves next. Cathal at 56 is the head of the Elders and his wife is only a year his junior. He isn't a large man the way Noah or Grady are being less than five foot ten, but his dominance is so strong that it makes him seem ten feet tall, and maybe a little bullet proof. He had been my father's beta and there was never a question as to why he held that position. His mate, Shea, is quiet and soft spoken on most occasions, preferring to sit back to take a room in instead of joining in, but if you can spark her interest in a topic you'll be treated to the fire that lays behind her gentle appearance.

After the Burkes come Elder Andrew and Lilith Cade. Andrew Cade always reminds me of a fallen angel with his dark hair, pale skin and sharp sculpted features. People who see Andrew would guess him to be vampire instead of the dark wolf he truly is. If Andrew is a fallen angel his mate, Lilith, would be an angel still in god's grace, with her pale blonde hair that is closer to white than blonde. Skin that has a soft ivory color and honest to god the woman has violet eyes. The only thing the pair is missing is contrasting black and white wings sprouting from their backs.

The last elder to approach is Elder Darius Arden and his mate Mae. Darius is an older black man with salt and pepper hair. The elder and his mate stand right around the same height, five foot ten. Mae is of Italian descent and has the olive skin to prove it.

Bloom invites all the elders to breakfast in our suite the next morning. Of course they all accept.

Once the welcomes stop Bonnie comes over and joins us.

She locks arms with Bloom and then looks at me and asks, "So Big Bad is it time for that tour?"

"Aren't you two tired? It has been a long day."

They look at each other and then back at me. Their faces remind me of children on Christmas morning, alight with excitement, anxious to see what the shinny wrapping paper will reveal. In unison they answer, "We're not tired!"

"Alright, give me a minute to call Tuck."

"Tuck?" Bonnie asks Bloom.

"Tucker. He's the oldest of my three brothers," Bloom explains.

"Oh yeah, so is he hot?"

"Bonnie!"

"Well is he or isn't he?"

"He's my brother!"

"He could be your hot brother."

"I thought you weren't going to get involved with members of the pack."

"I didn't say I wanted to be his mate and give birth to his pups. Geesh Blu, I just want to know if he is easy on the eyes." They're still standing with their arms locked together but now both of them have their other arms cocked on their hips and are staring the other one down.

"Bon …"

"Blu, is he eye candy or not."

"He could be considered attractive, if he wasn't my brother."

"Heck yeah!" Bonnie turns to me, "Alpha man, invite him to join our little tour. Oh or maybe I can get myself a private tour."

I dial Tuck's number and shaking my head say, "Sure thing."

Tucker picks up on the second ring, "Hey brother."

"Hey man. How's the Kyran situation going?"

"At the moment he's in town at the bar shooting some pool with his boys."

"Is Killian with him?"

"Nope, he's at home with mom. So how did the announcement go?"

"Better than it did the first time around. Bloom made arrangements for us to have breakfast with the elders in the morning. Do you wanna join us?"

"I think I'll skip this one, man."

"Understandable." Bonnie grabs my attention by waving her hands and mouthing "Tour! Ask him!"

I turn my back to her and sigh, "Man, the girls want a tour of the house and they thought you might want to join us."

"Why? I've seen it before."

"Bonnie has it in her head that you can be her eye candy for the night."

I hear Bloom giggle and Bonnie gasp. "So not cool Big Bad!"

Tucker asks around a laugh, "She calls you Big Bad?"

"Among other things," I grumble.

"I already like this chick. Is she hot?"

"Tuck man, my mate's standing right here."

"Sorry forgot man." He's silent for a second then continues, "But is she?"

"I doubt you'd kick her out of bed for eating crackers."

"Mmm, ok I'll be there in …" There is a loud crash in the background and a lot of hollering.

"Tuck, what's happening?"

"Shit man, it's Kyran."

"What the hell is he doing now?" I growl.

"He's starting shit with some of the older wolves."

"Do you need me to come put him in line?" I'm hoping he says yes, I've been aching to put that boy in line since his scene earlier today.

"Nah, I got this. Tell the girls I'll take a rain check on the tour."

"I will. Call if you need me, Tuck." There's another crash in the background.

"Shit, I got to go man before he tears down the whole damn building." Tucker is growling when he ends the call.

Damn Kyran, he's gonna make me break my promise to Bloom. If he keeps this shit up I will have to put him down, and he won't be getting back up. And that'll hurt my mate. Damn it!

I feel her hands on my arm as she presses herself to my back, "Tennessee, what's going on?"

I turn in her arms to face her, "Kyran's causing a ruckus at the bar in town."

"Do you need to go and handle him?" She asks softly, searching my face.

"No, Tuck is trying to get a handle on him." I push her hair off her shoulder and use my thumb to rub the freckle on her neck.

"Baby, I …" she looks away from me but she gathers her courage and turns to my eyes, "If you need to handle your business I won't hold it against you."

"Bloom …"

"No Pike, let me finish. I know you promised me but I see now that this is about more than me. He's putting others in danger now, right?"

I nod.

"All I ask is that you try to reason with him first. If he can't see reason, I promise I won't get mad if you have to …" She can't finish her sentence.

I circled my arm around her neck and pull her closer to me. Planting a kiss on the top of her head I whisper, "Darlin', that will be a last resort. We'll try everything we can to get through to him first."

Her hands are fisted in the front of my t-shirt, "I hope it doesn't come down to that."

"Neither do I, darlin'."

"I don't think I feel like a tour."

I look over at Bonnie, "Sorry, can I show you around tomorrow?"

She is watching her friend when she answers, "Yeah, that's fine." She turns her eyes to me, "Do you need me to help with anything?"

"No, Tuck has it under control."

"Okay. I'm gonna head back to my suite, if you need me don't hesitate to come get me." She's back to watching Bloom closely and I see how much she worries about her friend. My mate is strong, but today she has went through a lot of crap and it's taking its toll.

"Thanks, Bonnie," I call as she's walking away.

She turns and continues walking backwards as she replies, "Anytime." And I know she means it. She will do anything for Bloom anytime she needs her. She has moved almost 600 miles away from her family so her best friend won't have to face all of this alone. I hope she joins the pack; she'll make one hell of an addition.

I remove my arms from around Bloom's neck to grab her hand and inform her, "Come on darlin' I think it's time I take you home and tuck you into my arms for the night."

"Tennessee how is it that after such a short time you already know that that's what I need to wipe away all the bad that's happened today?" Her voice is barely a whisper and her eyes are shinning with unshed tears that I know she doesn't want to release. She doesn't want anyone in the pack to see her as weak so she's using all of her will to keep them from spilling down her cheeks.

Still holding her hand I lean in to whisper in her ear, "I know it because you're mine, and I'm yours.

Bloom, we may be two people in two bodies but our hearts and souls are connected as one. And thanks to that I will always know what you need to make your day better. And you'll know what I need to do the same for me."

"This mating stuff is pretty freakin' awesome."

"Yeah, it is," I agree trying unsuccessfully not to chuckle.

"Come on Tennessee; let's head home so we can get to the part where you wrap me up in your arms." She pulls back enough so I can see the grin that's lighting up her face.

"As you wish, darlin'," I say around a grin. Then I guide my mate back to our suite and hold her tucked into my arms the whole night.

Chapter 32 – Bloom

~ Unfinished business ~

Early that next morning I shoot up out of my sleep with a horrible sense of dread. I can't explain what I'm feeling. I just know something bad is going to happen. I try to recall the dream I was having before I woke up but I can't remember a single moment. Once I settle myself down and trample down the bad feeling (I don't want Pike feeling my apprehension through our connection), I get out of bed to begin preparing for the breakfast with the elders.

When I walk out of the bathroom I find Pike sitting on the balcony off our suite talking on his cell. I can tell by what's being said that he's talking to Tucker. When he sees me he tells Tuck goodbye and disconnects.

I walk to him and put my arms around his middle and my head on his chest and mumble, "Good morning."

He kiss the top of my head as he wraps his arms around me, "Mornin' darlin', I won't say good though by the way you were feeling when you woke up."

"Dang, I thought I hid it well."

"Nope, I caught it."

"Hmmph." I need to get this dang connection under control if I'm ever gonna have secrets again.

We shouldn't have secrets from our mate. My wolf chastises me. I, of course, ignore her.

"I understand you wanting not to worry me, but darlin' if these feelings are anything like the gut "feelings" you were having yesterday I need to know."

"I don't want to worry you over something that's nothing more than a bad dream," I confess to his chest.

"Even so, please share these feelings with me. I can at least hold you and help you through them if it's just a dream, but if it's something more we'll figure out how to handle that together."

"Alright," I concede.

"Thanks darlin'," he says using one hand to rub my back and the other to play with my hair.

"What were you and Tucker talking about?" I decide to change the subject.

He releases me from his arms and says, "We really need to go start breakfast."

"Pike, this sharing goes both ways." I step back and glare up at him.

"Okay, okay. Let's go into the kitchen and I'll tell you while we're fixing breakfast," He agrees then guides me to the kitchen.

I gather the ingredients to make pancakes and he assists by sitting on a stool at the island to watch me. I place the milk on the counter and tell him, "Get to sharing, Tennessee."

His elbow is propped up on the counter so his head can rest on his hand, but at my words he straightens and sighs.

"Kyran caused a huge scene at the bar last night."

When he doesn't explain any further I push, "What else? You already told me about that part last night."

"Well, he got to hollerin' at the people at the bar. Goin' on about how you're here to cause the pack problems and tear us apart. A couple of the pack members at the bar tried to calm him down but he took a swing at them, which lead to the whole bar ending up in a fight. Tuck, said that about half of the tables and chairs in the place were destroyed. Not to mention all the bottles of alcohol that was smashed and need to be paid for."

"Is everyone okay?"

"Darlin', they're shifters. They heal fast so that's not a problem and really neither is the damage, we'll have the money taken out of Kyran's account to pay for that. The problem is he got away from Tuck in all the uproar and he hasn't returned to his suite."

"He's probably somewhere sobering up."

"I wish you were right, but us shifters don't really get drunk darlin' so he wasn't hammered when he caused that mess and I doubt his feelings have changed where you're concerned."

"You can't get drunk?" I ask shocked.

"Nope, our metabolism burns off the alcohol too fast for it to affect us."

"Dang, do you think mine works that way too?" Hmm, so much I can do with that.

Heck yeah, it's party time. Finally my wolf and I agree on something.

"Not sure, but I don't want you going and trying to get plastered just to test it either."

Dang! My wolf and I say in unison.

"Oh alright," I begrudgingly agree. "Anyways, if the bar brawl isn't such a big deal then why do you look like you want to skin someone alive."

I dig through the cabinets to find the mixing bowls then I start to sift together the dry ingredients. When we came up with the idea of meeting with the Elders over breakfast Pike asked me make a list of groceries I'd need to cook for everyone (his fridge had been bare except for a carton of spoiled milk). I decided to fix blueberry pancakes, sausage, bacon, and some fresh fruit. He took my list and gave it to one of the pack members to pick up while we were getting ready for the pack meeting.

"Bloom, this is serious. He might try to hurt you." Pike pounds his fists on the island in frustration. I look up from sifting and see he now has a death grip on edge of the island. The nails on his hands have elongated into claws and are digging into the wood.

I look into his eyes and try to sooth him, "Tennessee, I'm his sister he won't hurt me. He may be confused by everything that's going on right now, but I don't believe for a second he'll hurt me."

He holds my eyes, "I heard your thoughts when you met him, darlin'. You saw anger and darkness and if last night was any indication that ain't gonna go away."

"Pike, we don't know if we can trust my gut," I plead.

He looks away, takes a deep breath and releases it before he meets my eyes again, "He took a broken bottle to Tucks stomach last night. Thankfully, it wasn't deep and we heal fast so Tuck's alright, but if he'd do that to one of his own brothers. He'd definitely hurt you and I'm not gonna allow it." Pikes words feel like a kick to my own stomach and I feel as if I can't breathe.

"Tuck …" I gasp.

"Darlin', I told you he's fine, but he agrees with me on keeping you away from Kyran."

"How are you going to do that?" His claws recede back into his fingertips and his face softens as he begins explaining the plan to me.

"We're banning him from the pack house and we're not letting you out in town without a guard. After the Elders leave I'm meeting with Tuck and the other men of the pack and we're setting up a guard rotation."

He scans my face. I know he's waiting for me to blow up. Hell, I want to blow up, but because I can feel him through our bond I know it upsets him to place these limits on me. So instead of screaming and accusing him of treating me like a prisoner, I take a deep breath and let it out then say, "Okay."

He gets up off his stool and comes to my side of the island. He kisses me gently then whispers, "Thank you darlin'."

"You can thank me by starting the bacon and sausage. We don't have long until everyone will be here and you bought enough meat to feed a small country." I push him towards the fridge that is holding the meat.

"Not a small country darlin', just a small group of hungry wolves." He turns from gathering the packages in the fridge to grin at me.

I roll my eyes at him and turn back to the island to start cracking the eggs. I hear him chuckle at me and send up a silent prayer of thanks that he's calmed down. For a second I thought I was going to have to hold him back from hunting Kyran down. My little brother is turning out to be a pain in my ass and if I didn't have to worry about keeping Pike and Tucker from ripping him apart I'd kill him myself.

We're sitting at the large table in the dining room off the living room. We finished breakfast an hour ago and just moments ago Pike and I finished telling the Elders the story of Rose and Dad's relationship, my growing up with no knowledge of shifters, to Pike finding me and what all has happened since. I take in the faces sitting around us. All ten have the same expression, confusion mixed with a whole lot of concern.

I start to think they've slipped into a bacon induced coma (they ate every last piece of what seemed like 10 pounds of bacon we cooked) and I'm wondering if I'll have to call around to find a doctor who specializes in reviving wolf-shifters from such ailments when Elder Andrews wife Lilith speaks up.

"Have you always been able to feel your wolf?" She's inspecting me closely with those striking violet eyes and I have to stop myself from squirming under her gaze.

"Um ... I didn't notice her until Pike came into the picture, but I think she's always been there just not as prominent as she is now." I hope that doesn't sound insane to her, but it's the truth. I have been thinking about my wolf a lot lately and the more I reflect back on my life the more I realize she has been in the background guiding me. But she has become a lot more vocal since Pike came into our life.

"Hmm that is curious," she mumbles as she exchanges a look with Elder Isla. I look between the two of them expecting one of them to speak what's running through their minds but neither speaks up.

"Please, if you have any idea what's going on don't keep it to yourselves," Pike begs apparently having caught the exchange between the two women.

"Pike, it's obvious why your mate's wolf has become more active since finding you, but I don't know of anything that would be keeping her locked inside," Isla semi explains.

"Why is she more active?" I ask watching Isla. She has her beautiful wavy hair pinned back at the sides with the rest falling loosely down her back. At my question she gives me a smile but it doesn't meet her eyes.

"My dear, isn't it obvious?" She asks back. I shake my head and she responds, "Bloom, you met your mate and his wolf is calling yours out. Just like Pike wants to be near you, his wolf longs to be near your wolf. So he's pulling her out of you."

"Do you think being around Pike when he actually shifts into his wolf will cause me to finally shift?" I ask trying to keep the hope out of my voice. Pike takes my hand and laces his fingers through mine for support while we wait to see what Isla's response will be.

"You've been around him in his wolf form and when he shifted back to his human form. If I understand correctly that is when his wolf started calling to yours. So being with him when he shifts to his wolf might be the final step you need to take to release her," Isla answers.

I look over at Pike and through our connection he says, *"If you want, darlin', we can try."*

"Tonight?"

He chuckles at my enthusiasm and answers, *"Yeah, we can try tonight."*

I smile at him and then turn my attention back to the elders who are watching us intently with smiles on their faces.

"I always love watching the newly mated. It's such a beautiful thing to watch fate bring together two souls who are clearly made for each other. Especially when those two souls are healing each other's wounds like you two happen to be doing," Shea Burke remarks watching us then swinging her eyes to her husband, Elder Cathal, asks, "Do you remember when you realized we were mates?"

I watch as the older wolfs imposing features soften and his eyes glimmer as he looked at his mate. He brushes her hair away from her temple and leans into kiss her there then answers, "Like it was yesterday. Your hair was pulled up on your head and you were wearing that oversized sweatshirt that hung off one side of your shoulders. You didn't have a scratch of make-up on your face and you smelled like lemonade. The moment I saw you I knew I'd never seen anyone more beautiful and I still haven't."

She is beaming at her mate's recollection of their first encounter. She leans into him and whispers, "I couldn't get over how much you smelled like leather."

"What's up with the scents?" I ask Pike through our bond. I'm still watching Shea & Cathal as I speak to him. It's reassuring to see them still so in love years after they first became mated. It gives me hope for Pike's and my mating.

"It's what draws a shifter to his or her mate. Only your mate can smell it and it's always something unique to them. It can also help you to find your mate if they were to go missing," he explains.

"And what do I smell like to you?" I ask shyly. I hope I don't smell like something gross, as much as I love Billy's pizza I don't want it to be the thing Pike smells every time he's around me.

He leans in and smells my neck, *"Strawberries and cedar,"* then he kisses his favorite freckle on my neck and pulls back to ask, *"What do I smell like to you?"*

I run my hand through his black hair and answer way to breathy, *"Like the forest after a rainstorm."*

"When can we expect to receive the invitations to your mating ceremony?" Fina asks reminding us we aren't alone.

"Umm," I look at Pike for help.

"With everything that's been going on we haven't had a chance to talk about it," he explains to them honestly.

"Now, don't be dragging your feet. Cementing your bond by doing the ceremony is just as important as everything else that has been happening," Fina scolds us.

"I promise Elder Fina as soon as we get the situation with Kyran settled, we will start making the plans," Pike promises.

"Good boy, just remember to give us ladies enough notice to find the right outfits."

"Will do." He chuckles at her then his expression turns serious when he says, "We've discussed Bloom's wolf now I'd like to know if any of you have ever heard of a shifter having these gut "feelings"?"

Everyone shakes their heads no and I have to sigh. I'm surrounded by people who can shift into wolves and I'm the strange one, it's disheartening.

Elder Darius speaks up, "We may be looking at this wrong. These "feelings" may not come from your shifter genes. Have you considered that it could be a trait you inherited from your father's side of the family?"

"My father never mentioned anything." I would've remembered if he had.

"It may be worth exploring," He suggests thinking he's being helpful.

"I don't have any relatives left on my Dad's side. My grandparents both passed away when I was young. Dad was an only child so no aunts or uncles. He never mentioned having any aunts or uncles himself, I always assumed my grandparents were only children as well," I explain the situation.

If Elder Darius is right and my "feelings" come from my father's side, I may never get the answers I desperately need. The whole situation is taking its toll. I slump into Pike's side for support and he hooks his arm around my shoulder holding me tight.

"Bloom, I promise we'll look into this to see if it could be you're shifter side. We won't shut that door until we're absolutely certain it's not part of your shifter genes," Isla vows.

"Thank you," I reply softly.

"You're welcome. Now I'm going to say something you may not thank me for, but it has to be said." I watch her, but don't say anything, as she takes a moment to collect her thoughts. She continues, "I understand that you don't get along with Rose, but you need to speak with her."

How can she suggest that after she heard my history (or lack thereof) with Rose? I open my mouth to respond.

She holds her hand up to stop me and explains, "I'm not saying become her friend. It's just that she was with your father for years, which means she was also around your grandparents. She may have experienced them having these "feelings."

She's right, I hate to admit it, but I need my mother for something. Damn!

I agree to talk to Rose and we thank them all for coming. Once they are all gone Pike offers to help clean up, but I know he has to meet with the men about guard detail. So I tell him to go on, that I can handle the clean up myself. He makes me promise not to leave the suite. I promise and he rewards me with a kiss then turns to walk to the door. I watch him pull out his phone and send a text, then he's out the door and gone.

I carry the dirty breakfast dishes into the kitchen, there aren't any leftovers to put away (the wolves were ravenous) so I rinse the dishes then load them into the dish washer. Once it's running I wipe down the counters and stove. The floor needs cleaned too so I search for the broom and dustpan then use them to sweep. I'm emptying the dustpan into the trashcan when I hear a knock on the door.

I set the dustpan beside the trashcan and lean the broom against the counter, then make my way to the door. My hand is on the knob turning it when I double over with the dreadful "feeling" I had that morning coming back full force. The door is pushed open by whoever is on the other side and I'm gripping my stomach still bent double. I look up to apologize for my behavior when the words die on my lips at the sight of Trace standing with Kyran. Neither of them look like they're here to apologize so I turn and try to run.

Trace hooks me around my stomach before I get two steps away and says, "Uh-uh my little flower, we have some unfinished business."

"Hurry up and knock her out, before she has a chance to contact him," Kyran growls from behind us.

"Fine," Trace grumbles clearly pissed that his play time is being cut short. "I'll see you soon my little flower."

I barely get the chance to yell for Pike through our connection before something is pressed to my neck and everything goes black.

Chapter 33 – Pike

~ Find Him. Kill Him. ~

The men are gathered in the meeting room and I'm explaining how the guard rotation is going to go when Bloom's fear hits me full force.

"PIKE," she cries out through our bond.

I don't even explain myself before I bolt from the room. I don't have to look behind me to know that the rest of the men are following me, they can feel that something is wrong.

I bypass the elevators and head straight for the stairs taking them two at a time. Our suite is on the top floor of the seven story building, it had once been a mountain resort, but the pack took it over 50 years ago and has kept it up to date since. The alphas suite has always been on the top floor, but at a time like this I wish I insisted on it being on the bottom.

I reach our suite and find the door standing wide open. I know she isn't there but that doesn't stop me from tearing through every room to double check. Her scent is strongest in the kitchen from where she's been in there cleaning and I can't make myself leave the room. I need her scent around me. I collapse against the island where she had stood hours before mixing up pancake batter and let loose a growl so loud that it shakes the cabinet doors, "GRRRRAAAAHHH."

Tucker approaches me slowly and bares his neck. I hadn't realized till that time that my wolf is in control. My nails have turned into claws and I'm holding on to my human skin by a very thin thread that's getting ready to snap. He takes in my appearance then says, "Alpha, we found Kyran's scent by the front door along with Bloom's and someone else that we can't recognize."

"Show me," I growl standing up and stomping back in the direction of the entrance to our suite.

The living room and hallway leading into our suite is filled with shifters in differing levels of their change. The lesser wolves completely shifted into their wolf forms when I had let loose my anger. They can't stop themselves from heeding the call of their alpha. The stronger wolves abstained mostly, some have their claws and teeth extended, but the top wolves like Tucker were able to refrain from the shift all together.

I pass them by without a word. My shoulders are back and my determined gait takes me swiftly towards the door. I know I'm pushing my dominance over everyone in the room I can hear the weaker wolves whimpering as I pass, but I don't have enough control of my emotions or my wolf to rein it in.

The scent of Bloom's fear hits me a few feet from the door. It's so strong that it washes out the other scent that I can tell is mixed in with it. Kyran's scent lingers just inside the door. I bypass it because I don't need to identify him, I know he helped and he's on my list for retribution. His sister won't be saving his ass after this foolish move. I lean in close to the door handle, where the unidentified scent is strongest and inhale deeply.

Yanking the handle out of the door frame I throw it through the wall across from the entrance and growl, "TRACE!"

"The human from Ohio?" Tucker asks from behind me.

I spin on him and grab the front of his shirt, "Yes! Find him. Kill him." Once my orders are out I can't control my shift any longer. I fall on all fours in my wolf form and let out a howl calling my pack to action.

Chapter 34 – Bloom

~ You gave me life again and the darkness went away~

My head is fuzzy and I'm not sure where I am. I can feel a scratchy blanket against my bare legs and I know my hands are handcuffed above my head. Opening my eyes and looking around I find myself in what has to be a rundown motel. There are two full size beds, each with ugly gold and burgundy blankets on them. That explains the scratchy material under my legs. Facing the bed is an off white dresser with an older television on top. The paint is chipped and some of the drawers are hanging in their slots crooked. To my left is a bathroom. I can tell by the light that has been left on that it's in desperate need of a scrubbing. To my right is a wall of curtains that hide me from the world outside and the door. It will be my only way out if I can find a way to get out of these handcuffs. I look up where my hands are bound and find the handcuffs are hooked through a metal circle in the light fixture right above the headboard.

There are voices right outside the door. Whatever is being said is heated, but I can't hear exactly what it is. Though I can tell it is Trace and Kyran. I have to get out of here, I don't know what Kyran is planning to do with me, but I know Trace is going to follow through with what he started at the lake. And this time I don't have Pike here to save me. Shit Pike, I can try to contact him through our bond. I've never done it with him being so far away and he's never told me if there are limitations, but right now it's my only shot.

"Pike, please say you can hear me." I repeat the same sentence over and over through our bond. My eyes are closed and I'm doing everything I can to concentrate on our connection.

Finally after what seems like hours, but is really just minutes, I hear his voice, *"Oh darlin'. Thank the lord."*

"Tennessee, Kyran and Trace have me," I start but I'm cut off by him.

"We know darlin'. I'm tracking your scent. Do you have any idea where you are? Are they there with you?"

"I'm in some run down motel, but I'm not sure where. They knocked me out before they took me. They're outside the door. I think they're fighting, but I can't hear what about. Tennessee, please hurry."

"I will baby. I think I may know the motel, we'll be there soon."

The sound of the door opening pulls me out of our connection and I turn to see my two captors standing there watching me.

Kyran looks me over then says, "Shit she's awake. I thought I told you to dose her again."

Trace looks me over too, but his look shows he clearly isn't upset about me being awake, "She's more fun this way."

"You moron, now she can contact him. She probably already has!" He screams and pushes the other man.

"Jesus calm down, it's not like she has access to a phone. Her fucking hands are cuffed." Trace pushes him back.

"I told you she doesn't need a phone. They are mates. They have a connection and can speak through it." Kyran steps back and begins to furiously fist his hands through his blonde hair.

"Fuck not that shit again, man. You keep that shifter crap up and someone will lock you away. I've known my little flower all her life. If she's a wolf then I'm a fucking fairy." Trace laughs at Kyran.

Kyran looks at Trace and me multiple times then says, "Fuck this! He's probably already on his way. I'm out of here." His eyes land back on Trace and he tells him, "If you're smart you'll pack her ass up and high tail it out of here too. Take her far away from here and keep her drugged and maybe he won't find you … maybe."

He looks back at me and I try to hold out hope that he'll finally see me as his sister and not his enemy, but his eyes are cold and uncaring and I know he'll never see me as anything other than the person who's tearing apart his family. He grabs a black duffle bag by the door and takes off, leaving me alone with Trace.

He shuts the door and locks it then advances to the bed I'm trapped on. His eyes slither up my body, making me wish I had dressed in layers instead of the sundress I put on for the breakfast with the Elders. He stops at the end of the bed and pulls off his dark green polo shirt. He kicks off his sneakers then drops his hands to the button of his khaki cargo shorts. He makes quick work of the button and zipper and they drop to the floor around his ankles.

I scoot myself further up on the bed, getting as close to the head board as possible. My legs are bent at the knees and I cross my ankles and gather my legs close to my body. He watches me struggle to get away from him and the more I do the larger his grin gets. He hooks his thumbs into the waist band of his boxers and I slam my eyes shut. I don't want to see his naked body. He laughs at my action and says, "I'll save that for later. Right now I want to play with my little flower."

I feel the bed give way under his weight as he crawls up the bed to get to me. He grabs one of my ankles and pulls me out of the protected position I've put myself in. I kick and buck trying to get loose of his grasp, but he's larger and stronger. He pins my legs down by straddling them.

"Pike, please hurry," I beg through our connection.

"What's going ..." he starts to ask but stops when he catches my thoughts and growls, *"That bastard is going to die!"*

Trace's hands climbing up my thighs tear me out of the connection. His fingers are skimming the hem of my dress and his voice is vibrating with pleasure when he whispers, "So beautiful."

I can't take any more. I can't allow him to do this to me. I jerk on my cuffs over and over screaming, "No, get the hell off of me." On the fifth or sixth yank, I feel the light fixture come out of the wall. It's still attached to my cuffs so I swing it at Trace's head. It connects with a loud crunch. I take advantage of his surprise and push him off of me. I scramble off the bed and back away from him.

He's holding the side of his head that's now oozing blood and cusses, "Fuck Bloom. What the hell?"

Is he serious? I glare at him, "You fucking kidnapped me and was planning on raping me you sick bastard!" I advance on him and swing the light fixture at his head again. I know I should be bolting out the door, but my anger has gotten the better of me and now I can't see pass wanting to cause him bodily harm.

The fixture connects on the opposite side of his head as the previous blow and he cusses me again, "Damn it, Bloom, stop!"

"Bloom, Bloom, BLOOM?" I scream my voice getting prominently louder with each repetition. "What happened to my little flower, huh?" He has both of his arms up trying to protect his head from any more damage as I continue swinging my make shift weapon and ranting.

"Your fucking flower isn't as weak as you hoped is she?" I sneer as I take a shot at his stomach. I'm so wrapped up in my revenge that I don't hear the door being busted in or the wolves that are piling in behind me. I just kept taking swing after swing at my kidnapper.

Traces arms fall away from protecting his head and his mouth falls open as he gasps, "What the hell?" His surprise gives me the shot I want so I slam the light fixture into his head again knocking him flat on his back.

"That's what you get you fucking asshole!" I scream at his prone body. Blood is seeping from the wounds on his head, but I ignore it and decide he needs kicked for good measure. I land one kick to his side before I feel strong arms circle around my middle. I begin to struggle and try to swing, but Pike presses his lips to my ear and whispers, "Darlin' that's enough. I'm here."

I sag with relief in his arms. He turns me so I'm facing his chest and holds me close as I bawl. He kisses the top of my head then twists his neck and orders, "Tuck, check to see if he's still alive. Price, see if you can find the key to the handcuffs."

I'm not sure if they nod or just get to their tasks because my face is buried in Pike's chest, but I know they are doing as ordered. Tucker moves to pass by us, but stops at my side to place a kiss on my temple. Then he leans into my ear and whispers, "I'm glad you're safe, sis."

I turn my face from Pike's chest so I can look into my brother's eyes and whisper back, "Thanks for coming to save me, little brother."

He looks over at the still unmoving form of Trace and says, "Looks like you saved yourself. Next time maybe you can save some of the fun for us."

"Tucker," Pike growls making me giggle.

"Okay, no next time geez." Tucker laughs then goes to check out Trace.

From behind us Price hollers, "I found them."

"Good lord, no need to scream just bring me the damn keys," Pike grumbles sticking out his hand for the keys.

"Sorry Alpha," Price says dropping the key into Pike's hand.

"It's okay, Price," he tells him then gently takes hold of my wrists and removes the cuffs. "How do they feel, darlin'?"

I massage my right wrist with my left hand as I answer, "Much better." With the handcuffs off and the adrenaline leaving my body I finally take notice of my mate. My eyes get large as I scan him from head to toe, "Tennessee, you're … you're naked!"

Price and Tucker laugh and Pike grins at me. "That's very observant of you, darlin'."

"Were you holding me naked?" I know my face is turning ten shades of red, which is making his grin grow impossibly wider.

"Yes."

"Why they hell are you naked?" I demand.

"Calm down darlin'," he tries to step closer but I step back and grab the blanket off the bed closest to us and threw it at him.

"Stop coming closer and put that on, geez, you could take an eye out with that thing."

Pike wraps the cover around his waist and laughs, "We're shifters darlin', you're gonna have to get use to nudity. We don't shift back fully dressed."

"We're designating a shifting zone in the pack house! I don't want to see a bunch of naked shifters running around all the time," I demand which gets me more chuckles from the three shifters in the room with me.

"We'll talk about it at the next pack meeting, darlin'." Pike tries to placate me.

"I'm serious, Tennessee!" I stomp my foot to get my point across.

He pulls me into his arms again and says, "I know, darlin'. We'll talk about it later. Now, let's get you out of here and back to the house."

"Okay, but shouldn't we call the law?" I ask turning my attention back to Trace's body. He hasn't moved or made a sound since the last time I connected with his skull.

"Price, go get Louie. Tell him to take over the scene and he can come to the house when he's done here to get Bloom's statement," Pike orders.

I look up at him and then at the door as Price exits and ask, "Who's Louie?"

"He's the sheriff and he's part of the pack." I let it sink in that the town sheriff is a shifter also and I can't come up with a suitable response. Pike gives me a squeeze, "Don't worry darlin', Louie isn't gonna to cover this up. You killed him in self defense and that will be put in his report."

"I killed someone," I say softly trying to bury my face in his chest.

He takes hold of my shoulders and holds me back so he can look at my face, "You protected yourself."

"But …" I begin.

"No darlin', I won't let you blame yourself for something he brought on himself. Twice he kidnapped you and attempted to …." He takes a moment to rein in his emotions then he continues,

"He attempted to rape you. I won't let you feel bad for defending yourself."

I place my hands on either side of his face, "Pike."

He covers my hands with his own and cuts me off, "No, Bloom. I won't let you."

"I wasn't going to fight you, Tennessee."

"You weren't?" He asks clearly surprised.

"No, I was just going to tell you I love you."

"I love you too." I pull his face closer to mine and kiss him letting our lips prove how much we mean to each other.

A cough coming from behind us pulls us apart, "Umm I hate to break this up, but I thought you might want reminded that your *brother* is in full view of your little show. And he really doesn't want to see his sister and his best friend trying to swallow each other's tongues."

I bury my face in Pike's chest to hide my laugh. Pike stares at his friend and says, "Get over it, brother. She's my mate and I'll probably be kissing her in front of you a lot."

"Okay, just saying you wouldn't like it if I was sucking on your sister's tongue in front of you," Tucker says holding up his hands in surrender.

Price walks back in and laughs, "You better not suck on Emily's tongue at all. Kit would skin you alive."

"I was just trying to explain the situation you two put me in when you latched onto each other at the mouth. I wasn't really going to make a move on Emily," Tucker grumbles as he stomps out of the room, apparently deciding he can't be around Pike and my show of affection any longer.

I can feel Pike silently laughing against me as he forces out, "Come on darlin', let's head home. We wouldn't want to sicken anyone else when we decide to become attached at the mouth."

"Stop being an ass!" Tucker yells from outside the room.

"Tennessee, stop messing with Tucker and take me home," I demand curling deeper into his arms.

"Anything you want darlin'," Pike promises placing a kiss to my forehead.

Louie came and interviewed me at our suite and Pike held my hand as I told him everything that happened from the time I opened the door till Pike pulled me into his arms at the motel. He told me that charges won't be pressed against me since I was defending myself. He also promised that they'd be searching for Kyran, and then he left Pike and me alone.

I took a shower to wash away the grime of the day and gave my sundress to Pike with the order to have it burned. After I got dressed, I join Pike in the living room on the couch. He pulls me into his side. I wrap my arms around his middle and lay my head on his shoulder.

"I've been in your life a little over a week and you've been in harm's way twice," Pike speaks to the room instead of looking at me. I can feel through the bond how he's blaming himself for my second abduction.

I let go of his waist and climb up to straddle his lap so we're face to face. I wait for his ocean blue eyes to meet mine and then I say, "Pike Lukas Masterson, just like you told me two hours ago, you will not blame yourself."

"Bloom, I shouldn't have left you alone."

"You will not go there. We all thought I'd be safe in this room and even after what happened I still feel safe here."

He searches my face and then asks, "How? After everything that happened here today, how can you still feel safe here? How can you still trust me to protect you?"

I position my hands on each side of his face and rest my forehead against his, "I know we've discussed this before but let me explain again. Pike, when you found me I was dying. There was nothing but blackness around me and an empty hole where my heart should've been. Then you showed up and you revived me. You gave me life again and the darkness went away. If I can trust you to bring me back to life after a year of being dead to the world around me, I have no doubts that I can trust you to keep the life you gave me safe."

Tears are streaming down his cheeks and his hands have a firm grip on my waist. He captures my mouth with his in a demanding, passionate kiss. My hands move into his hair to hold him tighter to me and we don't break apart until we are both desperate for air.

He's breathing hard when he says, "I don't know what happened in my life that made me deserve you, but I'd go through it all again as long as they guaranteed me I'd be on this couch in this moment with you."

Chapter 35 – Bloom

~ I think we have another mating coming on ~

"Darlin', Bonnie's here to see you," Pike hollers from the living room. It's the day after I was abducted and we've had almost everyone in the pack come by to check on me, including Kit and Emily. But I've been waiting on two people to show up and Bonnie is one of them.

I get up from the chaise lounge on our balcony and walk into the living room. She runs up and grabs me into a hug as soon as I've made it in the door. I hold tight to her and say, "Bon, I'm okay."

"If you ever scare me like that again I'll kick your butt," she tries to threaten but her voice is too shaky for it to sound convincing.

"I'll refrain from being kidnapped again, so you won't have to worry," I try to joke.

"Stop being a smartass, Bloom Michael! What would I have done without you in my life?"

She's barely finished her sentence when I feel the butterflies in my stomach start to go crazy. I look at my best friend and smile.

"Tennesse, I think we have another mating coming on." I tell him through our connection.

"Are you sure?"

"I'd bet money on it," I confirm confidently.

"I wonder who he is."

There is a knock on the door and I look at Pike and grin, "I think we're getting ready to find out." He doesn't say anything but moves down the hall to greet our new guest.

Bonnie looks at me and says, "Bloom, I don't like that look. It better not mean what I think it does."

"Don't worry Bon. I now know what you'd do if I'm not here."

"No, Bloom. I'm serious you can just tell that gut of yours to go to hell, because I'm not gonna be mated to one of the big bad." She's walking backwards away from me.

"Pike, you better hurry up and get whoever it is in here, because his mate is getting ready to jump out the window to get away from him."

He still doesn't say anything but I can hear his deep laugh coming through our bond.

"Who is it?"

I hear Pike's laughter coming from the hallway leading to the front door as he walks back towards us. Moments after he enters, still laughing, Tucker enters watching his friend like he's having a nervous breakdown.

"Sis, I'm not sure what's up with your mate, but you might have to have him committed," Tucker says shaking his head.

Bonnie who up till that point had still been trying to retreat from the room spins around and comes face to chest with Tucker.

He grips her arms to steady her and inhales deeply causing her eyes to grow to the size of saucers. He looks down at her and his voice is a growl when he states, "You smell like fresh apple pie."

"W-w-what?" Bonnie stutters still in shock.

He pulls her closer to his chest and declares, "You're mine."

That snaps Bonnie out of it. She steps back out of his arms and snaps, "I hate to tell you Fido, but I don't belong to anyone, especially not you. And I do not smell like freaking pie."

Tucker takes a step closer and she takes another step back, "You're my mate, Bonnie Anne Harris."

"How do you know my full name?" Bonnie asks stunned.

Tucker taps his finger to his temple, "We're connected now. You're my mate, Bonnie-bean."

She glares and pokes him in the chest with her index finger, "Oh no Big Bad, there will be no giving me pet names. There is no Bonnie-bean. There is only Bonnie and she is not your mate."

"Bon …." Tucker begins.

"No. You just need to forget it. I. AM. NOT. YOUR. MATE." She turns to me and says, "Blu, I'll see you later. Stay out of trouble."

"I'll try Bon," I answer trying to contain my laugh.

She turns to leave and Tucker grabs her arm to stop her. "Wait, we're not done."

She levels her icy stare on him and tells him, "Release me now, Lassie, or I'll make it so you can never produce children."

He releases her arm and looks at me for help.

"She's serious, little brother, her Daddy's a vet so she can follow through with that." I advise.

"Shit," he says running his hands over his face. While he does this Bonnie slips out of the suite and is more than likely half way back to Ohio to hide. Tucker looks at Pike (he has finally contained his laughter) and asks, "What the hell do I do now?"

Pike claps him on the back and informs him, "Now you go hunt down your mate."

"Pike, you just saw how she reacted."

"Tucker, a wolf like you should already know the best prey doesn't go down easy. Now go take down your prize, brother."

A wolfish grin spreads over Tucker's face and he stalks out of the suite to find his mate.

"Well that is an interesting revelation." I giggle.

"Yes, it is darlin'."

There is a soft knock at the door. "Come in," Pike hollers down the hall.

"Um …what's wrong with Tucker? He is stomping down the hall like a man on a mission." Rose asks from just inside the living room.

Pike looks at Rose then turns to me.

"It's ok, Tennessee. I need to talk to her anyways." I reassure him. He nods then takes a seat on the couch.

I join him and turn my attention to Rose, "Have a seat, please."

She hesitantly sits down and looks between Pike and me, "Is Tucker okay?" The concern for her son is sweet, but it hurts because I had been kidnapped and almost raped only a day before and she has yet to ask me how I am.

I swallow my anger and say, "Tucker is fine, he's just dealing with a …." I don't want to out Tucker and Bonnie's mating so I turn to Pike looking for help.

"He's got hunting on the brain," Pike assists.

"Okay, he should probably get out in the woods then," Rose mumbles.

"Rose, why are you here?" I cut to the point.

She fiddles with the hem of her skirt, "Well, Isla told me about yesterday. The breakfast meeting and what happened afterwards. Bloom, I'm sorry I would never have imagined my son Kyran capable of doing something like that."

"Rose, don't feel bad, none of us would've thought that. And I don't hold it against you." Though part of me wishes I can.

"Are you okay?" she asks softly. Maybe she does care a little bit.

"I'm fine," I answer her just as softly.

We all get quiet again, not sure what should be said next. I'm getting ready to tell her she should go when she speaks again.

"Isla, also mentioned your gut "feelings."" She hesitates to watch my reaction.

I hold my breath for two beats and finally release it and ask, "And?"

"Your father never had them that I know of," I visibly collapse till she continues, "but, I remember your grandma did. She would always say she had a "feeling" something was going to happen and whatever it was would happen. I always thought it was a coincidence, but if you're having the same "feelings" then there must be more to it."

"I guess I'll never find out what it is now," I sigh looking at Pike.

"I'm sorry?" Rose asks.

"They're all gone, Rose. Grandma, Grandpa, Dad, they're all gone. There's no-one left for me to ask about this," I explain calmly. I want to yell at her. She knows I'm alone. Why is she acting like she doesn't?

"Bloom, I'm sorry I know they're gone, but you still have family left," Rose informs me watching me closely.

"Rose, I know I have you and the boys, but they can't answer my questions about Dad's family."

"That's not what I mean."

"Then what did you mean?"

"Your grandma has a sister. She's younger than your grandma by several years and she's still alive," Rose informs me.

"I have a great-aunt?" I ask surprised.

"Yes, your grandma and her had a falling out when your Dad and I were in school, but she's still alive. Last I heard she lived in West Virginia with her mate."

"Wait, did you just say she has a mate?" I ask shocked.

"Yes, your father didn't know about that, but I overheard your grandma on the phone with her one day. Your great-aunt is mated to a shifter," Rose explains calmly.

I grab Pike's hand, "We have to find her, Tennessee. She may be able to give us the answers we need."

He squeezes my hand and says, "Looks like we're heading to West Virginia."

The end ... for now.

Enlightening Bloom Coming Winter 2013

Enlightening Bloom
By Michelle Turner

****These are unedited chapters that are subject to change****

Chapter 1 – Bloom
~Worth The Wait~

It's been a week since Rose sprung the news on us about my great-aunt. I wanted to leave right away but Pike (he always has to be the rational one) reminded me we had things we needed to do before we could take off again. The item at the top of his to-do list is why I am now standing in Bonnie's suite watching my white dress swish back in forth in front of her full length mirror.

Yep, he's making me go through with the mating ceremony before we take off. Okay, maybe he's not *making* me, but still you get the idea. He even used his Alpha voice when he informed me, *"We will not being going anywhere until you and I are completely bound."*

Which in case you didn't know in Alpha shifter speak means not only does he plan on marking me with his bite; he also plans on putting his ring on my finger and making me his wife. Now, I wouldn't be totally against this idea, but the way he went about the proposal pissed me off. Instead of getting down on one knee like a normal person to *ask* for my hand, I woke up one morning with the engagement ring already on my damn finger.

As you can see he's got a little controlling since I was kidnapped by Trace. But still he should've asked! And that's exactly what I yelled at him when I pushed his butt out of bed that morning. He of course thought my reaction was funny and knew I wasn't going to take the ring off so he got up off the floor and ignored my reaction as he asked, "So do you like the ring?"

The ring in question has a thin white gold band with diamonds running up each side until they meet a large tear drop shaped diamond at the top. He informed me he picked the tear drop shape to remind us both of the tear lined path that led us to each other. So instead of throwing the ring in his face, like I should've done, I leaned in and kissed him.

Yep, I'm a sucker!

Anyways, that's why I'm standing here looking at my reflection. Bonnie fixed my hair into lose curls and she pinned the sides back so it's all hanging loosely down my back exposing my neck and shoulders. Pike wants easy access to my neck and who am I to deny him when I love how it feels when he kisses me there.

Emily did my make-up since I'm a hopeless case when it comes to the stuff. She kept it simple with mascara, a light eye shadow and blush, and a soft peach lipstick and lip gloss. I'm starting to think she's a miracle worker, because I've never felt more feminine and beautiful.

"Blu, stop looking at yourself in the mirror and get over here to put your shoes on." Bonnie tries to reprimand me, but I can hear the smile in her voice.

I take one more long look at myself in the mirror to admire the beautiful dress I'm wearing. My white dress falls just below my knees. The bodice is made of satin and has a sweetheart neckline with a flowery bead design at my waist. The skirt flares out in to a bell shape and is covered in a flower patterned lace. Instead of the traditional pearls I'm wearing the diamond cross that my father gave me on my thirteenth birthday.

"I love you both." I say spinning around to face Bonnie and Emily.

"We love you too," they say in unison with matching smiles on their faces.

I run at them throwing an arm around each of their necks to pull them close. They both squeeze me tighter. Once we've all wrangled in the tears that are threatening to spill down our cheeks we pull back.

"Here ya go," Bonnie shakes her head, holding up my old brown cowboy boots. She's cleaned the dirt and mud off and they almost look new. For about a day Emily and her tried to talk me into high heels, but I wouldn't give in. I wanted my boots and being the new Alpha female I got my boots.

I pull them both on and look down at myself then back up at them.

"You're right. They're perfect." Emily concedes. Bonnie rolls her eyes, but since she's smiling while she does it I know she agrees.

"Here let's finish the look," Bonnie says as she hands me my small bouquet of blue hydrangeas and white roses.

As I take the bouquet there's a knock on the door.

"Come in." Emily hollers.

"Is the bride ready?" Billy asks peaking his head around the door. Billy flew in so he could walk me down the aisle. The ceremony is going to be relatively small consisting of the pack, Billy, and Bonnie's parents.

Holding my hand out for him I tell him, "I'm ready."

"You look beautiful, doll." He says coming in the rest of the way and taking my hand. A few weeks ago I would've been sad that my dad isn't here to, but since Pike's come into my life I've learned to live without that sadness hanging around. I know my father's in heaven watching me and he's happy that Billy is walking me down the aisle.

"Thanks, Billy." I kiss his cheek leaving my lipstick print behind.

"Does Pike look nervous at all?" I ask using my thumb to rub my lip print off his cheek. We decided to block each other's thoughts until I come down the aisle and I'm missing the feel of his presence in my mind.

"Not at all. Though if we don't get you out there, there's a good chance he'll come barreling up here to get ya." Billy chuckles.

Pike must be missing our connection too.

"Then we better not keep him waiting any longer." I laugh at the visual of my mate barreling up the stairs to get to me.

Billy holds his arm out for me and I place my hand in the crook of his elbow. The four of us walk out of the room and make our way down to the first floor. The wedding is being held outside of the pack cabin where the back deck overlooks the woods. Bonnie and Emily exit through the door before us and then the doors are closed leaving Billy and me alone.

"Your Daddy would be happy for ya," He whispers when he leans into place a kiss against my temple.

"I love you, Billy." I say in response.

"I love you too, doll." He says patting the hand that's holding onto his arm.

The doors in front of us opens and the sound of Keith Urban's song "Only You Can Love Me This Way" floats in from outside.

"Take me to my mate," I say smiling at Billy.

He guides me out on to the deck that wraps around the back half of the cabin. The wedding is set up on the right side of the massive cabin, because it has the best view. He leads me around the corner that leads to our guests and my future. I stop us at the back row of seats so I can search out Pike's eyes.

They're locked on me and he's smiling. We both open up our connection at the same moment.

"So worth the wait," he whispers through our bond.

Chapter 2 – Pike
~Officially Make You Mine~

"I didn't take that long, Tennessee."

"Darlin', I've been waiting on you for twenty-five years. Now get your beautiful self down this aisle so I can officially make you mine."

She continues her walk towards me, never once breaking eye contact. When Bloom and Billy finally make it to me, I take her hand pulling her into my arms and press my lips to hers. I hear the guests hooting and hollering behind us, but I'm not ready to break away from her.

"You're skipping the steps," Elder Cathal Burke chides me. He's the one proceeding over our wedding. It would traditionally be the Alpha's responsibility, but I can't proceed over my own ceremony so the responsibility fell to an Elder.

I pull away from the kiss, but I don't look anywhere but at Bloom when I reply. "Ok, you can start now."

"Today is a joyous day for our pack. Our Alpha is here to complete his mating bond and has invited all of us help them celebrate. Not only does he want to be bound to his mate by our ways; he also wants the outside world to know they belong to each other, so they'll also be reciting the human vows to become husband and wife." Cathal's voice booms over the wedding party. "Our couple is going to first recite the traditional wedding vows, and then they'll read their mating vows they personally wrote. Pike, will you please go first?"

I smile at my mate as I recite the vows that will connect us together in the human world. "I, Pike Lukas Masterson, take you Bloom Michael Daniels, to be my wife, to have and to hold, for better or for worse, for richer, for poorer, in sickness and in health, to love and to cherish, from this day forward until death do us part." Finishing the last line I stick my hand out palm up to Tucker and he places Bloom's wedding band there. I take Bloom's left hand and slip the band into place on her ring finger.

"Bloom, it's your turn." Cathal guides.

"I, Bloom Michael Daniels, take you Pike Lukas Masterson, to be my husband, to have and to hold, for better or for worse, for richer, for poorer, in sickness and in health, to love and to cherish, from this day forward until death do us part." She holds her hand out palm up until Bonnie places my ring into her palm. On a shaky hand she slips the band onto my ring finger.

"Pike, please recite your mating vows now." Cathal tells me.

Placing my palm to Bloom's jaw I use my thumb to trace her cheek bone as I recite my vows from memory. "Bloom, I was very young when I found out about mates. My father told me that a shifter's mate is made for him and him alone and that one day I'd find mine. Since that day I've been dreaming about you and when I found you I knew the real you completely surpassed the dream I had in my head all these years. You're more beautiful than a sunrise over a fall forest and sweeter than a berry picked ripe off the vine. But as beautiful as you are on the outside you're a million time more beautiful on the inside. You've shown me how much you care for the people around you, even when they haven't earned it and you've shown strength when most people would've had their spirit crushed. For all of this I promise I will always stand by your side to protect you, to support you, and to love you as my true mate."

I won't mark her until we're alone tonight, but at this moment I feel the need to lean in and kiss her neck right where my mark will be tonight. A shiver runs through her body and when I pull back I'm grinning. Bloom rolls her eyes at my grin and I chuckle so quietly I know only she will hear it.

"Bloom, it's your turn." Cathal tells her.

Taking my face in both of her hands she begins, "Pike, I never knew the world held love like this and if someone would've told me it did I would've laughed in their face, but from the moment you came running into my life I've seen it everywhere. In the way you love and guide your pack, in the way you love and care for your sister, and in the way you love and protect me. For opening my eyes to this kind of world I promise to always stand by your side, to always care for you, and most of all I promise to always love you as my one true mate."

As she finishes her words she tugs my face closer and plants her lips on mine. The wedding guests begin whooping and hollering again.

"I'm pleased to introduce your newly mated Alpha pair, Mr. and Mrs. Pike Masterson." Cathal shouts over the celebrating guests.

I pick Bloom up and spin her around, never letting our lips disconnect. Once I have her firmly back on her boot covered feet I throw my fist in the air to join in with the celebration. Out of the corner of my eye I see my beautiful mate shaking her head at me, but I know through our bond she's smiling while she does it.

I guide Bloom back up the aisle through the confetti our guests are raining down on us and back into the house. We stop just inside the door and I pull her into me for another kiss.

"Are you ready for the party, Mrs. Masterson?" I ask against her lips.

"Can't we skip the big party and go straight to the more intimate one, Mr. Masterson?" She whispers her question back.

"Don't tempt me." I rumble nuzzling into her neck placing light kisses there.

"Mmmm, if you don't stop Tennessee we'll never make it to the reception."

"Is there something wrong with that?" I ask pulling her tighter against my body.

"Down boy," She laughs as she attempts to push me away.

"Your husband is not a dog." I playfully growl at her.

"Wolf shifter. Dog. Same thing." She teases.

Scooping her up I throw her over my shoulder and swat her butt.

"For that I'm making you go to your reception," I tell her carrying her back outside where our guests are waiting under the tent that's set-up.

"Pike Masterson! Drop. Me. Now." She half scolds, half giggles as she wiggles around on my shoulder.

"Fine if that's what you want," I tell her as I slip her off my shoulder and smoothly maneuver her backwards into a dip. "Are you sure you want me to drop you?"

Gripping my arms she pouts, "No Tennessee, don't drop me. It'll hurt."

I scoop her back up into my arms and holding her close to my chest I promise, "Darlin', hurting you is the last thing I'll ever do."

She rewards my promise with a deep kiss, that's more suited for the bedroom then a tent full of guests, but I'm definitely not complaining.

The sound of Tucker coughing pulls us apart. "Are you two ever gonna come up for air long enough for us to congratulate ya?"

Bloom pulls back enough that we can look at each other then turning to look at Tucker we both say in unison, "No."

I bury my face in her neck to plant kisses and she giggles. In front of us Tucker turns to the rest of our guests and throwing up his arms announces, "Someone go get a crowbar. The love bird's lips have fused together and we need to get them apart so we can start this party."

Coming May 2013

PROMISED
By Michelle Turner

****These are unedited chapters that are subject to change****

November
Chapter 1 – Linc
~The Great Lincoln Tatman~

"I've found the girl of my dreams." I whisper to my cousin Nate.

"Oh, I have to see this. Who could possibly get the attention of the great Lincoln Tatman?" My cousin teases as he looks around the school parking lot.

"Shut it, smart ass." I use my shoulder to push him. He's been calling me that ever since I moved to town and all the girls at the high school started giving me the attention he use to receive. I've tried to explain to him that he can have it and those girls. I haven't found a single one that interests me, well until now, and she hasn't even looked in my direction. But Nate, being Nate, is pouting about not being the center of every girl's attention.

"Just point her out. I don't see anyone you haven't already had falling at your feet." He pouts pushing back on my shoulder.

"Over there." I point out a girl sitting under one of the large oak trees at the front of the school. She's leaned against it with her legs crossed, text book resting on her lap, and a notebook in her hand. I'm not close enough to make out the details of her eyes, but from here I can see how her curly brown hair is just passing her shoulders. I watch as it falls in her eyes for the fifth time since I've been watching and she uses the back of her hand to push it back in place.

She's wearing straight leg dark jeans and a pale blue sweater that exposes a small strip of her perfect stomach. She topped the whole look off with a pair of black high heeled boots that go to mid-calf. It's the middle of November and the weather is already feeling more like winter than fall so she really should be wearing a coat. I'm seriously thinking about going over and offering her mine. It would be the perfect opening to introduce myself.

"Ah hell that ain't happening." Nate laughs out loud beside me pulling me out of my perusal of the brunette.

"You think she's out of my league?" I ask puffing my chest out at what sounds like an obvious challenge.

"No man, that's not it at all. It's just that…" Nate stops, looking for the right words.

"Spit it out." I demand.

"Let's just say she doesn't date. Not *us* anyways." Nate says as an explanation shoving his hands in his pockets to keep them warm.

"Us as in me and you or us as in high school guys?" I question him.

"Linc, take my advice for once and drop it. Nothing will ever happen with you and that girl." Nate tells me looking me in the eyes.

"I think I can change her mind. She'd be worth it." I have no doubt about that. She's the definition of beautiful come to life. If her personality is a quarter of what her beauty is she'd be worth the challenge.

"See that Navigator pulling up?" Nate asks, but I don't see why he's changing the subject.

"Of course I do. I'm not blind." I snap.

"Watch it closely."

I do as he says. I watch as it pulls up to the curb a few feet away from where my dream girl sits under the tree. The doors to the black Navigator open up and four dark haired, muscled guys exit it. They approach my dream girl and help her gather her bag and books and then walk her to the suv. The one who is driving notices us watching them and glares at me as he slips back into the driver's seat.

"What the hell was that?" I turn back to Nate and ask.

"That is the best reason you have to stay away from that girl." He informs me.

"Brothers?" I ask.

"Extremely over protective brothers who are not afraid to rip off your man hood if you get within ten feet of their only sister." Nate clarifies.

"There are only four of them. With you at my back it might be an even fight." I reason out loud not ready to give up my dream girl.

"There were only four here today, but there's a fifth brother and a father. And her old man taught those boys everything they know so I wouldn't count him out of the fight."

"I doubt her dad is going to jump into the fight." I say doubting the description my cousin is using to sway me from the fight for my dream girl.

"Cuz, her dad is blood thirsty. He'd push his sons out of the way to get a shot at you. I hear he still bare-knuckle fights to earn some extra green."

"If that's true then he's crazy."

"Well my sources are very reliable so I'm warning you stay away from that girl and her family." Nate watches my face closely. Seeing that I'm determined to win the girl he says, "Fine I'll have your back. But if her old man kicks both our asses I'm telling my mom it's your fault."

"I'm not afraid of your mom Nate. Aunt Kelly is an angel." I climb in to my 1970 Dodge Challenger and say, "Come on I'll give you a ride home."

He crosses in front of the car then climbs into the passenger seat.

"You do realize Satan was an angel too, right?" He asks throwing his books into the back seat, which causes me to glare at him. He knows he's not supposed to throw his crap all over my car. My dad and I worked hard on rebuilding my Challenger before he was deployed and it means the world to me.

He rolls his eyes at me and leans back in the seat to grab his books. Once I'm convinced he's picked everything up I ask, "Did you just compare your mom to the devil?"

"Dude, you've never seen her pissed off. I swear the last time I made her mad two little red horns popped up out of her head and she grew a pointy tail." Nate exaggerates.

"What'd you do to make her that mad?" I ask backing out of the parking spot and pulling on to the road.

"I may have rear ended a cop car."

"What the hell were you doing that you didn't see a cop car in front of you?" I ask.

"I may have been checking out a girl who was walking down the street." Nate confesses looking out the window.

"Aunt Kelly should get a medal just for putting up with your crap." I state shaking my head.

"Hey! You didn't see this girl. Short shorts, long tan legs, and oh my lord she had on this top that was no bigger than a band aid. It barely covered her tits. You would've rear ended the cop car too." He turns to me as he pleads his case.

"If you say so." I have no doubt there was a hot chick but I highly doubt she'd be worth me getting in trouble for rear ending a cop car. Nate likes them hot, but he also likes them dumb. It's easier for him to fool around on them if they're not smart enough to catch on. Don't get me wrong I like them hot too, but I also want a girl with brains. I'm not saying she has to be the next Einstein, but I want to be able to hold an intelligent conversation with her. Preferably one not about her favorite lip gloss or which dress she looks better in. Seriously I actually had a girl talk to me for an hour about her favorite lip gloss. It was what I image torture to be like. If the terrorist ever needed to get some highly classified secret out of me they wouldn't have to water board me they would only have to bring that girl in and make me listen to her talk about whether she likes her Wild Watermelon or Berry Splash lip gloss better. I would spill every secret I know in two point three seconds flat.

"You know if it was Wyn walking down the road you would've done the same thing." Nate crosses his arms and stares out the window again.

"Wyn?" I ask him confused.

"How soon you forget your *dream girl*." Nate mocks.

"That's her name?" I ask gnawing at the bit for any information he can give me.

"You're not gonna forget about her are you?" Nate shakes his head.

"Doubt it." I admit honestly.

"Fine, but I did warn you."

"Noted. So spill."

"Her name is Arwyn Scott, but she goes by Wyn. She's the youngest of six kids. You saw the four oldest of her brothers. They guard her like she's the crown jewels and she doesn't associate with anyone at school other than the teachers." Nate tells me.

"No-one hangs out with her?" I ask thinking it's highly unlikely that everyone ignores a girl as beautiful as Wyn.

"Don't look at me like that. It's not like people haven't tried." He throws up his hands in defense.

"How long has she lived here?" If she has no friends she must be a new student too.

"She's lived here her whole life." Nate tells me.

"How the hell does she not have friends?" I ask getting mad. I'm imagining the stuck up kids at school shunning her because of her crazy family and I find myself wanting to defend her from them.

"She has friends they just don't go to school with us anymore."

"Oh my lord, could you be anymore cryptic. Just spit out the story Nate before I get pissed and make you walk the rest of the way home." I'm gripping the steering wheel so tight my knuckles have turned white.

"Damn, you're bossy today." I turn and give him the stare that clearly states not to try me.
"Fine! She had friends that went to school with us but they all dropped out. Most of them dropped a few years ago, that includes her brothers. They all dropped too. The youngest would've graduated last year I believe but he quit when he was around 14 or 15. I'm honestly surprised she's still in school. Her last friend, a girl named Dani, dropped at the beginning of last year."

"How the hell can a big group of students all drop out and have no-one care?" I ask stunned.

"Dude, they're Romani." Nate says thinking that explains everything.

"Romani?"

"Gypsies." Nate clarifies.

"Are you pulling my leg?"

"No Linc. Wyn is a gypsy as in the kind you see on those documentaries on TLC. Big puffy blinged out dresses and all."

Chapter 2 – Wyn
~The Black Sheep Of The Family~

"Dani?" I call out knocking on the door to my sister-in-law and best friend's travel trailer.

"I'm in the bedroom Wyn. Come on back." She calls.

I walk the short distance to the back of the trailer where the bedroom is located. Dani is sitting on the bed folding onesies and placing them into neat stacks in a wicker laundry basket. Her red hair is pulled up into a messy bun on top of her head and she's wearing black yoga pants and a tight fitting red tank top that shows off her tiny pregnant belly.

"So when will we know if I'm having a niece or a nephew?" I ask sitting on the edge of the bed and grabbing up a onesie to fold.

"The ultrasound is in three weeks." She tells me.

"Do I get to go with you?" I ask placing the onesie on the stack in the basket and grabbing another.

"I wouldn't have it any other way. I think Adam is going to take off and go too." Dani tells me smiling from ear to ear. All Dani has ever wanted since we were little girls running around my parent's front yard was to be a wife and a mother, and she always knew she wanted my brother Adam to be the man in that perfect life. Adam didn't realize Dani was the end all be all for him until sometime last January. But once he realized it he didn't waste time. He had his ring on her finger and her last name changed by April. They found out in September that they are expecting their first child and they've both been over the moon ever since.

"I think he's more excited to find out the sex than either of us." I return my friend's smile.

"He's so convinced we're having a boy he's already picked out a name and won't even discuss girl names." She says rolling her eyes.

"So what name has he chosen?" I ask.

"Clayton Allan." She tells me.

"He's not giving his child a name that starts with A? Complete blasphemy!" I tease. In my family everyone's name begins with an A, but my mother. My father is Allan (Al). Then there is my brothers Aidan, Aldon, Alec, Aaron, and Adam. Finally there's little ole me Arwyn. So Adam not going with the family tradition of choosing an A name might cause uproar in our tight knit clan.

"I know." She sighs. "I warned him what that decision might cause, but you know how these men can be."

"I'm proud of Adam for not giving into the family on this. Dani, you should be free to choose whatever baby name you want without having to worry about what my family might say."

"Even so, it's tradition." Dani states firmly.

"So have *you* thought about girl names? Since my brother is being a stubborn butt."

"If we do have a girl I'd like to name her Alana Arwyn." She says watching closely for my reaction.

I of course don't disappoint. I sit the onesie down and throw my arms around her giving her a hug, "You want to name your baby after me!"

"The middle name and only if the baby is a girl." Dani laughs hugging me back.

"Still, you are willing to permanently scar your baby with the same name as her black sheep aunt. I think that's a big deal." I pull back and smile at her.

"You are not the black sheep of the family." Dani scowls at me.

"I'm not married." I state.

"There are several Romani girls not married yet." She states firmly.

"I'm still in school." I fire off another reason why I'm the black sheep.

"Well." She's can't come up with a response to that so she sucks in her bottom lip and nibbles on the corner.

"It's ok Dani I know that I'm the black sheep of the family. And you know I'm exactly where I want to be. I asked Daddy to let me graduate." I try to ease her discomfort.

"I never understood that, but if that's what you want I'm glad he gave it to you." She tells me releasing her lip.

"I wish everyone was as understanding." I whisper to myself.

"I've got some news that will cheer you up." Dani declares putting her arm around me.

"Did you bake me the cupcakes that have sprinkles in the batter?" I ask. She knows I love the sprinkle cupcakes.

"No, but now that you bring them up I want some. I think this baby is going to like the same foods as his or her Aunt Wyn." She giggles.

"That's fitting since she's going to have my name." I grin.

"Only if it's a girl and it'll be her middle name." She corrects me again.

"I'm still calling her Lil Wyn." I inform her flicking my hand around.

"You are a complete goof." She laughs at me.

"So what the news that's better than cupcakes with sprinkles?" I ask getting us back on topic.

"I never said it was better than cupcakes with sprinkles. I said it would cheer you up." She reminds me.

"The only thing that cheers me up is cupcakes with sprinkles so if you say it'll cheer me up then it must be better." I explain my reasoning.

"I'm seriously re-thinking this giving my baby your name as her middle name. I don't know if I want her named after a goof." Dani kids.

"Oh hush! You know you love me just the way I am."

"There's no way I'd have you any other way." She gives my shoulder a squeeze.

"So what's this fantabulous news?" I ask turning to look at her.

"Rumor has it that Shay Dawson is planning on speaking with your Dad about your hand." She's so excited by this news she's bouncing her butt up and down on the bed.

"My hands seem fine." I try to play ignorant, because I so don't want this to happen.

"Oh don't even try that act with me. You know exactly what I'm talking about." She chides me.

"How reliable is this source?" I ask.

"Adam told me he heard it straight from Shay's mouth himself."

I let myself fall face first into the bed and grumble against the comforter, "Oh poop!"

"How can you not want this?" Dani asks as she absentmindedly strokes her pregnant belly.

"I'm not ready." I grumble against the comforter some more.

"It'll be fine." She promises.

"Do you know how soon he's planning his acquisition of me?" I sit up and snap.

"If Adam understood correctly, then it'll be happening soon." Dani tells me.

"Poop! Daddy promised me he'd let me finish school." I complain. I thought I had my Dad wrapped around my pinky about this. I thought he understood I wanted to finish school before I took this step, but if he entertains Shay's interest graduation could be thrown out the window. It's not that Shay's a bad guy, like Dani with Adam I've known him my whole life, but I don't see him like that. He's more like my sixth brother than my future husband. I don't know what the Hades has gotten into him if he's thinking about doing this.

"I better get home," I stand up and grumble.

"Ok, but you could stay a little while longer." She suggests.

"Nah, I need to get home and make some sprinkle cupcakes ASAP." I give her a hug and head out of the trailer.

As I'm walking out of the trailer I walk smack dab into my brother.

"Easy there Winnie." He says grabbing my shoulders to steady me. Out of all of my siblings I'm closest to Adam and he's the only one on this planet I allow to call me Winnie.

"Hey Addie." Just like his nickname for me, I'm the only one allowed to call him Addie.

"Leaving so soon?" He asks.

"Yeah, I'm gonna go make sprinkle cupcakes." I tell him knowing he understands the meaning of sprinkle cupcakes to me.

"What's wrong?" He asks releasing me. I'm about to answer when I notice we're not alone. A few feet behind him stands the reason I'm upset. Shay Dawson has his hands shoved in his pocket and is watching the exchange between my brother and me closely.

"We'll talk about it later." I tell Adam while I glare at Shay. I've decided he's on my list and he should know that's not a good place to be. If he thinks I'm going to roll over and take this betrayal easily he's sadly mistaken.

"I see Dani has been sharing." Adam says noting my glare.

"I have no clue what you're referring to." I try to play innocent turning my attention back to my brother.

"It's good to see you Wyn." Shay finally speaks up. He has taken one of his hands out of his pocket and is using it to smooth down his honey blonde hair.

"Don't even try it Shay Dawson." I snap my attention back to him.

"Come on Wyn. Don't be this way." He pleads.

"You….you..Ugh! I'm leaving." I throw up my hands and stomp off without saying goodbye.

Chapter 3 – Linc
~Your Future~

I'm sitting outside the counselor's office trying desperately not to think about Wyn. I haven't even spoken to her and she's the only thing I can think about. At lunch time yesterday I didn't see her in the cafeteria so I went looking for her. I found her sitting in the library reading another textbook and eating a sandwich. I was going to go over and talk to her but the school librarian caught her attention and I lost the little bit of nerve I had worked up.

"Linc, you can come in now." Mrs. Mandevers the school counselor tells me. She's standing in the doorway of her office and she moves out of the way to let me pass. I have just taken the seat across from her desk when I see Wyn walk in and have a seat in the little waiting area.

"Wyn, thanks for coming down. I'll be with you in a few minutes." Mrs. Mandevers tells her and then crosses to her desk leaving the door wide open so I have full view of my dream girl. I'll never be able to concentrate with her in such close proximity to me. I hope this isn't an important meeting.

"I know your new here this year and I thought we should discuss your future." Mrs. Mandevers informs me while she shuffles papers around in the file in front of her.

"Mmhmm." Is all I'm able to reply because Wyn's legs have caught my attention. She's sitting with them crossed and is bouncing her foot. Today she's wearing an oversized green sweater dress that falls off her left shoulder, a pair of grey leather leggings that cling to her perfect legs and a pair of green ballet flats that keeps slipping off her heel as she bounces her foot.

"So Linc what do you plan on doing with yourself after graduation?" Mrs. Mandevers asks.

I know the answer to this I've already decided to enlist after graduation, but because I'm so mesmerized by Wyn's legs I answer with, "I don't know yet."

"Well with your grades I'd suggest college. If you added a few extracurricular activities or community service you would have a good chance at some scholarships." Mrs. Mandevers jumps all over helping me figure out my life goals.

"Sounds good." I answer still not focusing on the conversation.

"Great. Here take these." She hands me a stack of applications and I look at them confused.

"Wyn, could you please join us in here." Mrs. Mandevers calls. I watch as Wyn gets up and comes into the room to take the seat beside me.

"What's going on?" I ask truly confused and nervous now. I should have paid attention.

"Lincoln Tatman this is Arwyn Scott." Mrs. Mandevers introduces us.

I look over at my dream girl who seems to be just as nervous as me and stick out my hand, "Hi, call me Linc."

She looks at my hand for a moment then tentatively places hers in mine and shakes it, "Call me Wyn, please."

This close I can see her eyes are a bright green and they are framed in the thickest, longest black lashes I've ever seen. And somehow I know they are not the fake kind girls buy, these are all Wyn.

I smile at her and nod my head. I don't want to but I release her hand and turn my attention back to our counselor.

"Wyn is very active in a local charity and helps out with tutoring here at school. I think she might be able to help you get involved in one or both of those so you'll have that to put on your college applications. Is that ok with both of you?" She looks between the two of us. I nod my head and I'm guessing Wyn nods hers, because Mrs. Mandevers smiles at us both and continues. "This is great. If you need any help filling those applications out come see me anytime. Linc let me talk to Wyn alone for a few minutes then she can come out and you two can work out your schedules."

I stand up and walk out closing the door as I do because I can tell they need privacy. I sit back down in the waiting area. My legs are bouncing up and down because I'm so nervous. I'm getting a chance to spend time with my dream girl, but now I'm worried

I'm going to mess it up. I've never in my seventeen years been nervous around the fairer sex, but one brown haired, green eyed girl has me quivering like jello. And she's only said four words to me.

To pass the time I look over some of the posters hanging on the walls. All of them are meant to inspire and encourage, but in reality they come across as cheesy. When the posters don't keep my attention long enough I pull out my cell to check my email. There's a new one from Dad and I open it.

From: Andrew Tatman
To: Linc Tatman
Subject: Missing You

Hey kiddo-

Mom told me you got all A's and B's the first nine weeks and I can't be prouder. I hear your cousin is being a pain, but try to ignore him. He'll grow up eventually and when he does he'll regret the way he's acting. Don't let his childish behavior push a wedge between that special relationship you two have had since you were kids.

Mom also said you brought up a girl the other day. If she's caught my boy's eye she must be something special. You're like your old man in that sense, not just any girl can turn a Tatman's head. It has to be the really wonderful ones like your Mom. I want to hear all about her.

I hope you're taking good care of the Challenger. Make sure you check her oil regularly and don't be racing her. I know how tempting it can be at your age to want to show off, but it's dangerous. So don't!

I should be back home in time to watch you graduate. So get prepared to spend some quality time with me. I'm missing our weekends on the lake.

Well I better get off here. Don't forget if you need any advice on this new girl to shoot me a line, I'm sure I can come up with something good to tell you.

Like always, take good care of your mom and I'll write as soon as I can. I miss you both like crazy.

Love,
Dad

A single tear slips down my cheek just as the door to Mrs. Mandevers office opens and out steps her and Wyn. I quickly wipe it away and shove my phone back in my pocket. I miss dad terribly and as soon as I get home I'm going to reply but right now I need to focus on the girl in front of me.

Mrs. Mandevers looks me over to make sure I'm okay, apparently having caught the tear, then deciding I'm fine looks at Wyn, "Please think over what we discussed."

"I will, but you know I can't promise anything." I can hear the disappointment in her voice. Whatever it is they talked about she wants to do it but for some reason she can't.

"Good. Now you two exchange information and let me know if you need me. I'm going to get back to work. Have a nice day." She smiles at us both then walks back into her office and shuts the door.

I stand up and rub the back of my neck. "So where do we begin?"

"I guess we should exchange numbers." She says looking everywhere but at me.

"Sounds good." I pull my cell back out of my pocket and hold it out to her. "Here's mine, program your number in and I'll put mine in yours."

"Um, ok." She pulls her phone out of her book bag and hands it to me. I quickly type in my phone number and save it.

"So when should we get started on this?" I ask exchanging our phones back.

"Well I do tutoring after school on Wednesdays and I volunteer at an after school program for kids on Tuesdays and Thursdays. It's up to you which one you'd like to join." She tells me putting her cell back in her bag.

"Well I'd love to come and help today but I have to go home and help my mom. Is tomorrow okay? And maybe next week I can come to the tutoring too." I tell her.

"That's fine. Tutoring was cancelled today anyway." She pulls out a tablet of paper and a pen then scribbles down an address and hands it to me. "Meet me at this address after school tomorrow."

"I could give you a ride there tomorrow if you want." I tell her taking my wallet out and putting the piece of paper in there.

"That's a nice offer, but I can't. I'll meet you there." She says putting the paper and pen away.

"Well do you need a ride home today? I really don't mind."

"My brothers should be here by now. So no thanks." She says pulling the strap of her bag onto her shoulder and walking towards the exit.

"Well at least let me walk you out. I'm going the same way." I say following after her.

She stops, looks me over then sighs, "Linc, it's nothing against you but I'd prefer you didn't. It will cause me and you all kinds of problems if they see us together."

"Wyn, your brothers don't scare me."

"That's good because they aren't bad guys. They just have their ways and I don't want you drug into what those ways entail. I promise I'll meet you tomorrow, but please for me stay here until I'm out those doors." She pleads with me.

As much as I want to argue with her I can't. Once she has me drawn into those green eyes and pleads with me in that silky smooth voice to do something for her I have no way of telling her no.

"Fine, but do you mind if I text you later if I have questions about tomorrow?" I ask knowing very well the texts I'll be sending won't have any questions about volunteering.

"That's fine I guess." She gives in. "Bye Linc. I'll see you tomorrow."

"Bye Wyn. I'm looking forward to it." I give her my smile that more than one girl has referred to as drop you to your knees gorgeous.

She returns my smile and I must say her smile is ten times more potent than mine.

About the author:

Michelle is a 28 year old native Ohioan. Go Buckeyes! Who now lives with her husband and son in West Virginia. When she isn't spending time with her family you can find her with her nose stuck in a good book. She released her first book (Reviving Bloom) as an independent author in October 2012 and plans to release two new books (Promised & Enlightening Bloom) in 2013.

To find out more information on Michelle and her upcoming projects check out these addresses:

Facebook: https://www.facebook.com/MichelleTurnerAuthor

Blog: http://michelleturnerauthor.blogspot.com/

Pinterest (check out the Reviving Bloom & Promised boards to see how Michelle pictures her characters): http://pinterest.com/michelle8605/

Made in the USA
Lexington, KY
20 August 2013